Casper's Courage

By the same author

Top Gun For Hire

Casper's Courage

DEREK TAYLOR

A Black Horse Western

ROBERT HALE · LONDON

© Derek Taylor 1999
First published in Great Britain 1999

ISBN 0 7090 6592 2

Robert Hale Limited
Clerkenwell House
Clerkenwell Green
London EC1R 0HT

Typeset in Liverpool by
Derek Doyle & Associates.
Printed and bound in Great Britain by
WBC Book Manufacturers Limited, Bridgend.

*With thanks to David Barnes and
Derrick Lawson, two old-timers*

ONE

Deadeye, his bad eye at right angles to his nose and trying to go farther, was as drunk as ever and would not be happy until his Colt .45 was out of its holster and smoking. Will Casper had watched him for some time, wondering when the action would start.

'You've had enough and I ain't serving you no more,' the bartender said, removing Deadeye's glass and wiping the spot on the counter where it had been.

That was it, the excuse Deadeye had been waiting for. Staggering backwards, he went for his gun.

'No one refuses me a drink.' His gun was out and his aim surprisingly straight. He'd have hit the bartender had not a shot from Will Casper's own Colt sent his gun spinning out of his hand.

'What the. . . !' Deadeye exclaimed, turning to see where the shot had come from.

Will Casper stood defiantly, gun in hand. Then he spoke. 'Deadeye, like all the towns you've ever holed-up in, this one's had enough of you. Now get before you're got.'

Swaying some, Deadeye tried to focus his unruly eyes on the man whom he reckoned was behaving a mite over-bearing.

'You the sheriff or something?' he asked.

'Nope but I don't need to be. Now are you gonna get?'

Deadeye reckoned he had no choice. He was without a gun and the man, whoever he might be, wasn't playing. Steadying himself in drunken fashion, he put one faltering foot in front of another and took his leave.

Holstering his Colt, Will Casper threw a look of malevolent satisfaction around the bar. Everyone remaining knew who he was and most reckoned he was best left to his own devices, which were more than sufficient to keep a man alive in the lawless Black Hills of Dakota in the years of the gold-rush.

Will Casper had drifted into the Dakota

Territory from Wyoming on a westward tide of hopefuls reckoning to strike it rich in the gold-fields. Prospecting, though, hadn't suited him and he soon discovered his talent for shooting fast was highly prized in the mining-camps. He was working now as a shotgun messenger for the Cheyenne and Black Hills Stage Company.

Downing the last of a beer, he reckoned it was time he hit the sack in readiness for an early morning start undertaking some urgent business for his employees. Making his way through a scattering of tables at which men were gambling and drinking away their pickings, he had a notion Deadeye hadn't entirely ceased to be a problem yet. People gave him the nod as he passed by them but his steely blue eyes hardly showed he'd seen them.

'Thanks, Will,' a grateful bartender called out to him as he drew close to the batwing exit. Casper acknowledged this by raising a hand and gesturing with a finger.

It was summer but the night was pleasantly cool. Will Casper turned and walked down a rough and not too firm boardwalk towards his hotel. Out of the light of the saloon, the night was lit only by a half-moon. But Casper did not need eyes to tell him that someone had stepped on to the board-walk behind him. Without hesitation, he stopped and turned to face Deadeye head-on.

'You still here?' he asked.

'If you ain't the sheriff, I don't see what busi-ness it is of yours,' Deadeye replied.

Casper could see that he'd armed himself with another gun. Looking at him, he despised him for everything he stood for. He was not just a drunk who pissed away every nugget of gold he found; he was troublesome with it. And now he thought he was tough.

'You make it my business by causing a distur-bance where I'm having a quiet drink.'

'Well, maybe you oughta drink somewhere else,' Deadeye replied.

'Is that so?' Will Casper remarked. Deadeye was rolling some on his feet. 'Maybe you oughta try and make me,' he added.

With that he began to step towards Deadeye. This and the fixed look on Will Casper's face, which became more visible to him as he drew closer, unnerved Deadeye. Slowly his addled brain began to tell him to draw. But it was not quick enough. Will Casper drew when he was only two steps away from him.

'Your kind makes me sick Deadeye. Go drink in hell.'

Will Casper drew his Colt and thrusting it straight into Deadeye's belly, pulled the trigger.

'What?' was the only word that issued from Deadeye's lips as he fell to the ground clutching a stomach that was pouring blood and undigested beer and whiskey chasers.

'You heard,' Will Casper said, as he turned to continue the walk to his hotel and a night of sound, unbroken sleep.

The next morning as he was collecting his mount from the livery stable, he was side-tracked by the town's sheriff, who wanted to know if he'd had any part in the shooting of Deadeye. There were no witnesses but it was obvious to everyone what must have happened.

'Sheriff, if you want to take me in over a low-down, drunken skunk, fine. You do your job but there could be consequences,' was Will Casper's answer.

The sheriff, being mindful of Casper's reputation for deadliness was in no hurry to test it.

'Will, I just want to clear up the matter. The whole saloon says that Deadeye was spoiling for a fight and was drawing his gun on anyone he took a fancy to. Anyone that did shoot him down did it, no doubt, in self-defence, and that's where the matter will rest. I just need to know, that's all,' the sheriff replied.

'Good. Well now you do,' was all Casper said, indicating the conversation was closed. Pushing on, he left the sheriff standing, relieved that it was as far as anyone would expect his enquiries to go.

As Will Casper rode out of town, he was glad to think he'd done what the Cheyenne and Black Hills Stage Company paid him to do. Deadeye wasn't a robber of stagecoaches, but his type was more than a nuisance to folk that were passengers on them. His mind, though, didn't dwell on Deadeye for long; there was other more important business the company wanted him to get on with. In the last few weeks a number of stages had been held up en route from Deadwood to Rapid City, seemingly by the same gang. The company wanted him to find the gang and bring them in dead or alive. They were offering a big bonus on top of his already high wages. It was his plan to trail the stage from a distance as it made its daily run that day. It had already left town. At a prearranged place, he'd meet up with a sidekick,

Sam Willard, and together they'd ride hard to catch up with the stage. Then from high ground above the trail they'd keep lookout.

He rode his bay at a steady pace and covered the ground from town to the meeting place in good time. He arrived just in time to find Willard pulling up his mount. The two men greeted each other and after a few minutes were on their way at a gallop to catch up with the stagecoach.

As they rode over hillocks and across wooded slopes, with the higher reaches of the Black Hills behind them, both men kept an eye out for gangs of Sioux braves. Indians themselves didn't pose much of a threat these days, but there were some renegade bucks who thought they were still living in the heady days that followed Custer's defeat at Little Big Horn River.

At last the stagecoach came into sight. Seeing it, Casper and Willard pulled up their horses.

'There she is,' Casper said.

'What now?' Willard asked.

'We keep out of sight but follow her until she's within reach of Rapid City. If they're gonna rob her, it'll be between here and there,' replied Casper. 'She's carrying a shipment of prospector gold. Word's probably out about that.'

The sun was still high in the sky. Both men were cool in their buckskins but the going was tough. Another thirty or forty miles and they'd be able to ride with the stage into Rapid City. Casper was beginning to think no one was going to show this time, when from the east he saw a gang of six men come riding out from behind a clump of trees.

'There they are,' he said to Sam Willard.

'Didn't think they'd let a chance like this pass them by,' was Willard's reply.

It wasn't long before the man riding shotgun messenger on the stage realized what was happening and began to aim lead in the gang's direction. This activity up front kept the gang from noticing what was going on behind them. Casper and Willard had given rein and were now riding hard to catch up with the gang. When they had them in range they opened fire with their Colts. Hit by rifle fire from the stagecoach, one of the gang fell from his horse. A bullet from Casper's Colt winged another.

He kept his mount but only after a heroic struggle. The leader of the gang quickly realized there was fire coming from in front and behind and pulled his horse off the trail. Turning his fire on Casper and Willard, he led the gang west across

14

the hills. In hot pursuit, Casper and Willard were gaining on them when Willard took a bullet in the shoulder and was thrown from his horse. Casper could see that he fell badly and knew he had no choice but to stop. Firing a last shot at the gang, he reined in his bay and quickly rode to where Willard was lying. Luckily Willard had not broken any bones but he didn't look in a state to get back on his mount.

'Sam, can you ride?' Casper asked, some moments after getting Willard into a sitting-up position and giving him some water from a canteen.

'Don't worry about me, Will, get after that gang. Don't let 'em get away.'

'They've already done that. Best we can do now is ride back and see if we can find the one that was shot. He might still be alive,' Casper replied.

After a few minutes, he helped Willard get to his feet and on to his horse.

'You ride on,' Willard said. 'If that cowpoke is still alive, you don't want to go letting him get away.'

Casper looked doubtful.

'Go on,' Willard insisted. 'I'll be all right.'

15

TWO

Dunc Blackman led the gang that had got away. He soon realized the chase was off. To be sure, he rode on some distance before pulling up. He guessed who it was who had led the chase. Will Casper's reputation had spread far and wide through the Black Hills. He'd always supposed it wouldn't be long before they had him on their backs.

'What now, Dunc?' Ace Ruben, one of his men, asked.

'There'll be other stages and if they're carrying gold we'll be ready for them,' Blackman replied. 'In the meantime, we'll deal with Casper. Ace, Tom, come with me. We'd better go back and see if Joe's dead or alive.'

'Do you think that's wise, boss? I mean, Casper could reckon on us doin' just that and be waiting for us,' asked Ace.

'Well, we can't just leave Joe where he fell. Wouldn't want us to leave you, would you, Ace?' was Blackman's reply. 'Billy, Josh, you two ride in a circle and come back on the trail some. If you come across Casper, fire a shot and we'll know. We'll go back the way we came.' With that, the gang split up.

Blackman and his two long riders spotted Casper and Willard first. Willard was obviously finding the going hard and both he and Casper were walking their mounts. Seeing an opportunity not to be wasted, Blackman opened fire immediately and Ace and Tom followed suit. Casper saw immediately where it was coming from and spurred his bay in the direction of some cover immediately on their right. In an instant he was firing back and a lucky shot killed Tom. Blackman and Ace rode their horses into the cover of nearby trees and a gun battle ensued. Hearing it, Billy and Josh set their mounts in the direction from which the sound of gunfire was coming.

'Leave me, Will, there's too many of them,'

Willard said. He was barely able to hold himself up.

'Shut up, Sam, I ain't going nowhere. At least, not without you. Just fire when you can,' Casper replied.

Both sides kept up a barrage of rifle and hand-gun fire. Billy and Josh soon joined Blackman and Ace. Blackman cursed them for not taking cover where they could set up some deadly crossfire, but reckoned that's why he was leader and they followers.

'We're gonna run out of ammo,' Willard remarked.

'And so are they,' Casper replied. 'But I've still got plenty of rounds left.' He took careful aim with his Model '73 Winchester. Billy peered out from behind a tree and Casper's shot took away a lump of his head.

'And what I've got I'll make count,' he added levering down the trigger to put another bullet in the breach.

'Dunc, I reckon we oughta ride. He's too good,' Ace called to Blackman.

'Shut up and keep firing, Ace,' Blackman replied. 'We've got him outnumbered.'

'Yeah, but we ain't killed him yet, nor even hit him.'

Just then a bullet from Casper's Model '73 took a large chunk out of the tree behind which Blackman was standing. Feeling splinters of wood strike his face. Blackman quickly returned fire from his Remington carbine. He was a good shot, but not the crack shot Will Casper was and he knew it. Josh was about to say that he agreed with Ace, when a bullet ripped into his chest, fatally wounding him.

'God damn it!' Blackman exclaimed, coming out from behind the tree and firing a number of shots one after the other into the place he knew Casper to be. But none hit home. Shots fired in anger usually went wide of their mark. Casper's carefully aimed return fire sent more splinters flying into Blackman's face. Blackman began to think that Ace was right.

'Come, on then,' he said to him, after a few seconds' reflection. 'I ain't got many rounds left, anyway.'

As the firing ceased, Casper could see what was happening. He watched the two men creep away and let go a few more rounds in their direction, but stopped when they swung up on their mounts and began to get away behind the cover of the trees. He knew he'd just be wasting lead.

'Go on, ride, you lily-livered bastards! Ride!' he called after them. Then he turned his attentions to Willard, who looked barely conscious.

'Ain't there no one that can get you, Will?' Willard uttered, as Casper put a canteen to his lips.

'There ain't been no one so far,' Casper replied.

After making sure Willard was comfortable, he set about getting the dead men strung across their horses. He hadn't, he knew, got all the gang, but he reckoned he'd got a few dollars' worth of them and he aimed to trade them in.

Dunc Blackman cussed as he made his getaway. In one day he'd lost all but one of his men. There were others in the gang's hideout but those who had been lost were the cream of the bunch and it was going to be darn near impossible to replace them. When he felt the distance between him and Casper was wide enough, he pulled up, with Ace following suit.

'Reckon we've got some unfinished business,' he said.

'Yeah,' was Ace's reply.

'Where do you reckon Casper's gonna head? Deadwood?'

'I don't see where else he'd go. That was Sam Willard with him and he sure as hell needs a doctor,' Ace said.

'Well, maybe that's where we oughta head. I don't reckon he saw our faces. We could get him there.'

'Perhaps it'd be better to go and get the rest of the boys and ride into town tomorrow.'

Ace had had enough for one day. He knew Casper's reputation, they'd just had proof of it, and he was still reeling from losing men he counted as his friends. He needed time to come to terms with the fact.

He thought for a moment. 'It'll soon be dark,' he said. 'If Casper sees us riding into town after what's just happened, he might put two and two together and come up with the right answer. I reckon we oughta just lay low for a while. Maybe even wait for another stage carrying gold. Casper will be expecting us to try and rob it. We could set a trap for him then.'

'Yeah, maybe you're right,' Blackman reluctantly agreed, adding, 'We'll go back to camp. But I ain't gonna feel happy until that son of a bitch gets what's coming to him.'

THREE

It was dark by the time Will Casper and Sam Willard rode into Deadwood with their cache of dead outlaws. They pulled up their mounts outside the Cheyenne and Black Hills Stage Company agency office. Casper was helping Willard to get down from his horse, when one of the company's employees saw them through the window and rushed out.

'Will, Sam, what happened?' Jim Niven asked.

The telegraph had not come to the Black Hills yet and news of the attempted hold-up of the stage had not reached Deadwood.

'This bunch of no-gooders tried to hold up the stage and Sam got wounded,' replied Casper. He'd got Willard off his horse and was supporting him.

'Here give me a hand to get Sam into the office and then go and fetch the doctor. He's lost a lot of blood.'

'Sure thing, Will,' Jim Niven replied. 'Is this all of them?' He was looking at the four dead bodies thrown over the horses.

'All except their leader and one other.'

They got Willard into the office and sat him down.

'Now go get the doctor,' Casper ordered. 'Hang on, Sam,' he said turning to his sidekick, 'the doctor will be here in a minute. I'm gonna go find the sheriff and trade in that vermin out there.'

Casper could have wished that 'Wild Bill' Hickok was still the sheriff of Deadwood, but he wasn't. He was dead, shot in the back a year or more past. They'd tried to get Casper to pin the badge to his chest, but he didn't like the idea that you had to please half the money in town to keep it there. He preferred dealing with outlaws in his own and the company's way. That way you avoided the scheming niceties of the law, which usually failed the decent citizens of town and succeeded for the villains.

He found the sheriff in his office.

'Evenin', Fred,' he greeted Sheriff Brown, as he walked in through the door.

'Why, good evening to you, Will,' the sheriff said, getting up to greet a man he held in more than high esteem, and some trepidation. 'What can I do for you?'

'I got four members of the gang that's been holding up the stage. They're all dead. Reckon them's your property now,' Casper informed him. He gave the sheriff the low-down on the attempted hold-up.

'So you say two got away? Did you get a look at them?'

'No. We didn't exactly get to kissin', Fred. That'll have to wait till next time,' Casper replied, thinking it was typical of the kind of fool-hearted questions the law asked.

Without saying any more, Casper took his leave of Sheriff Brown. He was hungry, he was thirsty and never much interested anyway in the law and its enquiries into his way of doing things. Looking in on Willard to make sure the doctor was there doing his best to see that he didn't die, he headed for the sleazy part of town.

Gold-fever had created Deadwood and gold-fever filled the coffers of its tradesmen and vict-

uallers. The saloons and hotel bars were full of
people drinking, gambling and whoring. Will
Casper did his fair share of all three. This night
his blood was high and there was only one way of
cooling it. Word had got out that he had brought
back to town dead stagecoach robbers and a man
he bumped into wanted to buy him a drink to
thank him.

'Casper, you're a mean-hearted son of a gun but
you done right bringing in those bastards and I
for one want to thank you,' said Dan Cruze, one of
the more successful prospectors. 'What you drinking?'

'Beer,' was Casper's reply.

They pushed their way to the bar and Cruze got
him a large glass of frothing beer. Drifting away
from Cruze, Casper began to cast an eye about for
Miss Melanie, in whose house of ill repute he was
standing. He saw her standing by a card-table in
a large alcove off the main room. He knew the
men playing at the table. They were all big shots
in town. Life's opportunists, they'd all come to
Deadwood on the back of the gold-rush and were
making a killing. Miss Melanie's back remained
towards him until he touched her. Then she
turned round.

'Why, Will, honey, it's good to see you,' she said. She was a stunning beauty and, dressed in the finest silks, she was a picture of elegance and style seldom seen amongst women on the frontier. She'd been Bill Hickok's girl once, now she was his. It told you the kind of man she liked. 'You look done in. What say I fix you a hot bath?'

Casper indicated that he couldn't think of anything he'd like more. They went to her private suite of rooms and on the way she issued orders that hot water was to be fetched.

'So who was it this time? Did you recognize them?' she asked.

'No, I didn't get close enough, but I daresay it was the same old crowd, just served up differently,' replied Casper.

'Persimmon Bill?' suggested Melanie.

'Maybe, though I don't think he'd have given up so easily. Whoever it was, they'll be back for more and we'll be waiting for them. This town ain't ever gonna amount to anything with the likes of those vermin running wild.'

'Deadwood itself is pretty wild,' remarked Melanie.

'Yes, but it's on its way to becoming something.

And that bunch of thievin' sons of bitches is delayin' it.'

As Casper spoke, the air outside the saloon filled with the sound of gunfire, and not for the first time that day. They looked at each other and laughed. In the next instant they were in one another's arms. The bath had been filled with hot water but it was a good twenty degrees less hot by the time Casper fell into it. While he bathed, Melanie dressed and went back downstairs to the saloon to check on business. Casper, when he was washed and dressed, went to check on Willard. He found Niven in the company's office alone.

'Where's Sam?' he asked, looking around and seeing only blood where he'd sat him down.

'He didn't make it, Will. Doctor Berger said he'd lost too much blood. I had him taken down to the undertaker's,' Niven replied.

Death was no stranger to this frontier town, but it was bad when it was a colleague gunned down in the line of duty. Niven's face reflected this.

Casper wasn't surprised to hear the news. Few men on the trail survived a bullet in the chest and a rough ride back to town. His hatred of road agents and their gangs knew no limits. The fact that one of them had taken another good man's life filled him with bitter anger. He hadn't ridden shotgun for a while. He decided he'd do so on the next stage out of town.

'Jim,' he said, 'we carrying gold to Cheyenne tomorrow?'

'Sure are, Will, and about twenty thousand dollars in cash, too.'

'Right. I'll be riding shotgun. I want McManus and Wright riding inside. With a Remington apiece.'

'There ain't no room. We got a full complement of passengers,' Niven replied.

'Well, two of them will have to ride on the next stage,' Casper instructed Niven in peremptory tones. 'Explain to them why. They'll understand. If necessary give them a refund and tell them their next passage is free.' As he finished speaking more gunfire erupted in the street. 'Reckon Sheriff Brown might need a helpin' hand tonight,' he remarked. In the mood he was in he didn't care who paid for Sam's death. All gunnies were the same to him. One of them tonight would be picking up the tab.

He turned and stepped out of the stagecoach

office on to the boardwalk. He checked his Colt for bullets.

FOUR

Dunc Blackman was sitting at a table in a deserted prospector's cabin perched on a ledge over a gulch in the Black Hills above Deadwood. He had no ideas of panning for gold; it simply made for a good hiding-place. Men posted as look-outs could see anyone approaching for miles.

It was late and Blackman was thinking of turning in when a familiar sound signalled to the look-outs that a friend was approaching. It was Davey Divine, who'd just come hotfoot from Deadwood. He had information for Blackman and hurried into the cabin to tell him.

'There's a stage leaving tomorrow for Cheyenne and it's gonna be carrying a shipment of gold and a lot of cash. I heard it being talked about by a couple of the company's messengers who was called out of the Number Ten. I followed them and heard them being told Casper was going to be riding shotgun and they were to ride inside with the passengers,' he informed Blackman.

'Nice work,' Blackman remarked. 'Send Ace in to see me.'

'Sure thing, boss,' Divine replied. As he went to leave the cabin, he turned and asked, 'How many of the boys riding?'

'All of them,' Blackman replied firmly.

A few minutes after Divine's exit, Ace stepped into the cabin. He and Blackman discussed the news Divine had brought from Deadwood and then talked about where best to attack the stage. They decided they'd lay in wait at the Canyon Springs relay station along Beaver Creek.

'We'll need to get there early,' Blackman concluded. 'Tell the boys we'll leave at sun-up, sharp.'

Casper's dark mood had not left him overnight, despite helping Sheriff Brown rid Deadwood of one or two more of its undesirables. The only payback that really mattered was that to be paid by the surviving members of the gang that tried to rob the

Deadwood to Rapid City stage the day before. As he made his way from the structured part of town through tent city to the staging-post, he secretly hoped he'd get the chance to avenge Willard's murder before the day was out. He arrived at the company office to find the stagecoach and horses rigged, ready and heavily guarded. McManus and Wright were in the office checking over their hardware and supplies of ammunition. McManus, a deadly looking giant of an Irish immigrant, was checking the barrel of his Remington.

'Let the thievin' bastards come within range of this,' he said to Casper, as he entered the office, 'and I'll blast them to kingdom come, so I will.'

Casper threw him an approving look and then asked Jim Niven, who was busy with paperwork, if the gold and cash were all loaded.

'Good morning, Will,' said Niven. 'It is and there's a lot of it, which is why we're using the Monitor.'

'So I noticed,' Casper remarked. 'Which means a change of horses at Canyon Springs.'

The Monitor was an iron-lined strongbox on wheels. In the absence of a key, it would take a sledgehammer and crowbar to break open its doors.

'It does, but they'll be ready and waiting for you on arrival,' Niven replied. 'These are your two passengers,' he pointed at two men sitting on a bench at the front of the office. One was a mining engineer returning to home and family in Montana, while the other was a prospector carrying his own gold to Cheyenne en route to Texas where he intended to set up a cattle ranch. They both took comfort in knowing the man riding shot-gun messenger was none other than the most noted shooting man of them all, William D. Casper.

'It sure is good to know you're gonna be riding up top,' the mining engineer said to him.

'Wouldn't feel safe with anyone else,' echoed the prospector.

Casper acknowledged their praises with a nod of his head, saying, 'The company does its level best to get you from A to B without let or hindrance. When you're ready, McManus, Wright.'

McManus and Wright collected up their armoury of firearms and followed Casper out to the Monitor. It was going to be driven by Gene Barnett, who was on top, setting the stage's six reins.

'You near ready for the passengers?' Casper called up to him.

'About so,' Barnett called back.

'Right, then,' Casper said. 'Let's load 'em up and move 'em out.'

When the passengers and armed guards were loaded and the paper-work stashed, Niven secured the Monitor's door with a huge padlock.

'There you are,' he said to Casper, throwing him the key. 'Don't lose it!'

Casper caught it in mid-air and locked strong fingers around it. Inside the Monitor, Wright pushed a number of bolts into place.

'Good luck, y'all!' Niven called out, as Barnett shook the reins to set the Monitor rolling.

Dunc Blackman led his men out of their hide-away. He took a last look over his shoulder, wondering if he'd see it again. Not that he loved it so much, but that he knew if he did not return it would be because he was dead.

Shrugging off such thoughts, he dug his spurs into the sides of his horse's belly.

They rode a fair distance, before coming within sight of Beaver Creek and the track that would take them to Canyon Springs relay station. The day was going to be a fine one and the landscape was magnificent. Even Blackman could appreciate this.

'Doesn't it make you feel glad to be alive?' Ace remarked to him, as they slowed to cross a stream.

'Yeah, and that's exactly what I plan to stay, alive,' answered Blackman. 'I wish Tom and Billy were with us. I don't like riding with novices, untried men.'

'They're all right,' Ace said, throwing back his head to indicate the six men riding in double line behind them. 'They've survived plenty of scrapes of their own.'

'Maybe,' said Blackman, 'but I got a bad feeling about this one.'

'Then why do it?' Ace asked.

' 'Cause we need the money. And besides, it ain't superstition. If I got a bad feeling, it's because I don't feel surrounded by men I can trust.'

Ace wanted to laugh out loud at Blackman's unease, but didn't dare. His boss was always nervous before a hold-up.

'Boss,' he said, 'it only takes one gun to do the damage and yours is usually it. The rest of us is just there to make a frightening noise.'

What Ace said made Blackman laugh out loud.

'Yeah, he grinned. 'Guess that's just about it.'

By now they'd reached a spot just above the relay station. They pulled up their horses and Blackman studied the scene and assessed the situation.

'Divine,' he said, 'I want you to ride into the place and scout about a bit. Make it look as if you're just riding through. Normally, there's only a stock-tender looking after the place. If there's more than one of them, signal by taking off your hat and mopping your brow. Stay out in the open and we'll see you.'

'What then?' Divine asked.

'We'll be prepared,' Blackman said.

Shortly after, Divine was tying his horse to the hitching rail in front of the relay station cabin. A wiry old stock-tender came out to greet him.

'Howdy, partner!' he sang out, holding a loaded shotgun, his finger on the trigger, the barrel decently low but ready to be lifted. 'What can I do for you?'

'I'm just passing through,' Divine smiled. 'You got any grub? I'm pertnear starved to death. And so's my mount. Got chased by Injuns and lost my saddle-bags and bedroll.'

'Is that so?' the stock-tender asked, not sure he

could believe a word the man said. He looked
pretty cool for someone who, if he'd been chased
by Indians, would have needed to be Wild Bill
Hickok himself to have escaped. And he didn't
look no more than a common cowpoke. 'Where you
up from, then?'

'Oh, Texas. I heard there's gold in these parts,'
Divine replied. He stepped out into the open, from
where he knew Blackman could see him. 'You
suffer from Indian attacks here?' he asked.

'Nope. I don't suffer nothin' here,' the stock-
tender replied.

'You all alone?'

'Yep. Most of the time, though the stage calls in
here twice a day. Once going and once coming.
One's due in about an hour's time.'

'Is that so?' Divine said, stepping about and
looking as if he was stretching the stiffness of a
long ride out of his legs. His hat stayed firmly on
his head. 'Been here long?' he asked, walking
towards the cabin and mounting its steps.

'Long enough,' was all the stock-tender said in
reply. He wasn't happy about the stranger but
reckoned he couldn't keep him standing outside.
'Well, if you're hungry, I guess I can fix you something to eat. I ain't much of a cook though.'

'That's all right,' Divine replied. 'I ain't fussy.'

Though not one to entirely trust strangers, the stock-tender nevertheless led him into the cabin. He turned to tell Divine there was coffee on the stove. As he did so Divine drew and shot him. It was the simplest solution, he thought, and cleared the way for Blackman and the others to ride on in.

The Monitor rolled on steadily towards Canyon Springs. Being steel-lined and full of gold and men, it weighed heavily on the backs of the team of six pulling it. For all intents and purposes, it looked like an ordinary stagecoach but everyone knew what it was. Casper kept his eyes peeled for trouble, though he knew the likelihood of an attack before they were well clear of town was negligible. It was a beautiful morning, with the prairie rolling away into the vastness all round them and the Black Hills looming high above.

'What do you think, Gene?' Casper asked. 'Do you think they'll try and rob the stage today?'

'It must be mighty tempting, Will,' replied Barnett, a man of few words.

'Yeah,' said Casper. 'Well, we'll be ready for them.'

Casper's Courage

*

Dunc Blackman never questioned Divine's actions in killing the stock-tender. 'Get that corpse outa here,' was all he said to him, on entering the cabin and helping himself to a mug of coffee. Half an hour later he told Ace it was time to put the men into place. 'Tell them to lie low until I give the word. Everyone stays outa sight until I open fire and then all firepower is to be concentrated on Casper. Once he's out of the way, the rest'll be easy.'

As the minutes ticked by, the air became thick with tension. Every man knew of Will Casper's legendary status in Dakota Territory. Still fresh in all their minds was how he'd fought off Blackman and Ace and killed Billy and the others, almost single-handed. Men like him seemed to have a ring of impenetrable armour around them, like the knights of old. Only fools and desperados ever risked taking them on. As the sun rose higher in the sky all that could be heard was the buzz of insects and the occasional snorting and hoof-play of the horses in the corral. The gang's own horses were out of sight behind the cabin.

The Monitor was heard before it was seen. Right on time, it came rolling heavily into the relay station, trailing clouds of dust behind it. Tugging on the reins, Barnett pulled the team of six to a halt. Casper jumped down from beside him, intending to put the wheel-blocks into place.

'Lorrie, you here?' Barnett called out, wondering where the stock-tender was. Manning a relay station was a lonely job and usually the stock-tender was there waiting to greet the stage the moment it appeared. Casper's eyes darted everywhere. What he couldn't see, he could sense.

'Where is the man?' Barnett asked.

Divine's trigger-finger itched, as he watched Casper go behind the low-slung wagon. 'He's guessed,' Blackman thought to himself.

'There's something wrong,' Casper said, looking up at Barnett, who was still sitting in the driver's seat.

'Yeah, where is that son of a gun?' asked Barnett.

'Gene,' Casper said, 'when I give the word, get this thing moving and get it outta here.'

Inside the Monitor, Wright and McManus could hear what Casper was saying.

'Casper,' Wright called out, 'what is it?'

Before Casper had a chance to answer, Blackman smashed a cabin window with his rifle butt and started firing.

'Go, Gene, go!' Casper called out to Barnett.

In an instant Barnett had the horses moving. Lead seemed to be coming from all directions, thumping into the Monitor and whistling about his head. Casper took cover behind the stage-coach, running alongside of it as it gathered speed.

'What the hell is going on?' McManus called firom inside.

'Reckon that's obvious,' Casper called out over the din the Monitor made as it rolled along. It was soon going too fast for him to keep up, and with one leap he pulled himself up on top.

The manoeuvre to ride on out of the relay station had taken Blackman and his gang completely by surprise. They'd let rip with a storm of lead but all of it became wide of the mark as the Monitor was driven round a clump of trees in the yard of the relay station and onwards down the trail.

Blackman soon ran out of the cabin. 'God damn it, stop firing, stop firing!' he called to everyone, taking off his flat-topped Stetson and mopping his brow.

Ace was the first to appear at his side. 'What now?' he asked.

'God damned son of a bitch!' Blackman exclaimed. 'It almost makes you think he was expecting us, the way they suddenly hightailed it out of here.'

'Ain't we gonna give chase?' Ace asked, as the other men began to gather around them.

'I don't think so,' Blackman replied. 'Casper would probably pick us off one after the other. He's got a long journey ahead of him. There's time enough yet.'

Barnett kept the whip cracking until he was happy the horses were going as fast as they could. Inside the stagecoach McManus, Wright and their passengers were having the ride from hell. On top, Casper was looking out for the gang. It soon became apparent to him that they were not following. He took a few minutes to make absolutely sure, before calling out to Barnett to halt the stagecoach.

'Halt, did you say?' Barnett called over his shoulder. With all six reins and the whip in hand, he needed every last ounce of his considerable muscle power to remain in control of the situation.

'Yeah,' Casper shouted back. 'They ain't following.'

Relieved, Barnett brought the Monitor to a halt. McManus, Wright and the passengers let out a collective sigh of relief.

'You all right in there,' Casper asked, jumping down.

'What do you think?' McManus asked. 'Just let us out of here, will ya, Will?'

As Wright slid back the internal bolts, Casper fished deep into a pocket and pulled out the key Niven had given him. In a second he had the padlock off and the three men inside tumbled out.

'What in God's name happened back there?' Wright asked.

'Someone was lying in wait for us,' Casper replied. 'Can't think why they ain't followed us though.' He looked back down the trail. 'Reckon one of you had better ride on top with me. I don't believe we seen the last of that bunch of no good sons of bitches. If they ain't chasing us now, they sure as hell are gonna be chasing us later.'

'I'd sure like to know which gang it is,' Barnett remarked.

'Reckon you will soon enough,' was Casper's reply.

FIVE

Barnett kept the Monitor going at a steady pace through the outer shells of the Black Hills and into the rolling hills of Four Corners, heading for the way station in Newcastle. Wright and McManus took it in turns to ride above with Casper. Casper didn't expect the gang to try anything along this part of the route to Cheyenne, simply because the terrain was not right for it. Red rock buttes and ponderosa ridges greeted the eye whichever way one looked. There was no open country and the trail was narrow and restricted. Still, he kept a sharp eye peeled for any eventuality. Dusk was falling as they drove into Newcastle, men and horses alike near done in.

'Sure am glad to see you folks,' Dan Davis, the

man in charge of the way station, greeted Casper and the stagecoach crew as they alighted and dusted themselves down.

'Feeling's mutual, Dan,' Casper replied.

Hearing his words, Davis looked at the stagecoach, and where bullets had thumped into it and said, 'You ain't been robbed, have you?'

'Pert darn near! At Canyon Springs. They was lying in wait for us,' Barnett said. 'Casper here got us out of it.'

Casper was about to return the compliment, but Davis interrupted, asking if they'd come across Indians.

'No, never saw a one of them,' Barnett replied. 'Why?'

'There's a war party on the rampage. Soldiers came in today to warn us,' Davis informed them.

'We had troubles of our own,' Casper said, then asked, 'Any strangers show?'

'Nope,' replied Davis.

'Good,' said Casper. 'Wright, McManus, secure the stage. Davis, show our passengers here some of your good hospitality. Sorry you had a rough ride, folks. Maybe tomorrow it'll be easier. We'll be on our way at sun-up.'

'That's all right, Will Casper,' the prospector

sang out. 'Reckon we got you to thank for being alive.'

'And Barnett,' Casper replied modestly, turning and walking towards Newcastle's only hostelry, a log cabin. 'Don't forget Barnett.' Indians, he thought, as if we didn't have troubles enough already.

Once in the log cabin, he headed straight for the bar and grabbed a bottle of redeye. The next morning, his head still thick from downing all of it, he picked a couple of good-looking short horses from the company's stock-pen and had them saddled up. He decided Wright should ride shot-gun with Barnett, while he and McManus should act as outriders, keeping a lookout not just for road agents, but now for Indians, too. They set off with Dan Davis exhorting them to watch out.

'You'll probably come across the army,' he called out to them. 'There's a whole company of them camped up at Hat Creek station.'

'The army!' Casper scoffed. He'd had little respect for their approach to the Indian problem since Custer made such a hash of things and got himself killed at Little Big Horn. If there was a war party on the rampage, he knew that unless they wanted to be found, the army were the last people on earth who'd be able to track them down, much less deal with them once they had found them. Indian women and children, yes, they could find them easily enough, but Indian renegades, that was another story.

The day was going to be a scorcher. Already the skies were turning to blue, as they began to follow the trail through a vast expanse of sagebrush and short grasses criss-crossed with small streams. Casper and McManus rode a mile or more in opposite directions out into the prairie, scouting for signs of human activity in a landscape that should otherwise have shown little trace of it. But its vast openness could be deceptive, especially where the trail rolled down to the broad muddy basin of the Cheyenne River. In fact this was an area fast earning the name of Robbers' Roost. Cover could easily be found in the flood plains where there were forests of cottonwood, and along the river's course where there were steep banks. As the trail dipped towards the river and its many tributary rivulets, the driver had also to make sure he had the stagecoach fully under control, as it plunged into the mud or the raging torrent of the waterway itself.

Casper knew the Monitor must be nearing the

basin of the Cheyenne and was beginning to head
for where he knew it must be, when he caught
sight of what he reckoned could only be men
riding. They were coming in fast at an angle that
would take them straight into the path of the
Monitor. But were they Indians or were they the
gang that had tried to rob the stage at Canyon
Springs? Casper couldn't tell yet. His mount was
good and still fresh; he decided he'd take cover
until the horsemen were close enough to identify.
Once he could gauge who they were, he'd decide
on his strategy. Whatever, he reckoned he could
outrun them, if the need arose.

Blackman and his gang were riding hard. He'd
intended to lie low south of Newcastle but had got
lost trying to cut the trail late in the day and had
ended up miles off course. This had become apparent to him and Ace only after sun-up the next day.
They had cursed, wishing that Tom, who knew the
prairie lands of Dakota Territory like the back of
his hand, was still with them. But he wasn't and
they'd ridden around some time before getting
their bearings

Watching them fumble their way, though unbe-
known to them, was the Indian war party, twenty
or more of them, all Sioux. They knew who and

what the gang were and guessed what their intentions might be. Their plan was to let them rob the stage and then rob them afterwards. They rode now at a safe distance in a line that would converge with Blackman's when the time was right. McManus had spotted them, but, like Casper, didn't know who they were. His response was to hightail it to Casper and see what he reckoned. They were still a long way off, which would give him time to reach Casper.

Casper saw McManus come galloping towards him. The horsemen kicking up dust in the distance seemed no closer and he guessed they wouldn't see McManus.

'Casper, I see'd horsemen riding fast from the east in our direction,' McManus told him.

'From the east?' Casper asked, looking west and seeing the men he'd spotted. McManus's eyes followed his.

'You sure they're not the same men?' Casper asked.

'Sure. I was on the other side of the trail and they was coming from the east. These are not the same men,' McManus insisted.

'So which is which?' Casper mused out loud. 'Which the Indians? Which the road agents?'

'Too far to see, Will, but they're both heading this way and that can only mean one thing,' McManus replied.

'You ain't wrong, Pat,' Casper agreed. 'It'll be the gang that tried it at Canyon Springs who'll rob the stage and it'll be the Indians who try and rob them. It begins to look to me like that bunch out there is the outlaw gang. They're riding pretty tight. Indians ride loose. I'll hang on here a bit longer to make sure. You ride back to the Monitor and warn Barnett and Wright. Tell Barnett to go hell for leather for the river and to get across it.'

'What about the Indians?' McManus asked.

'Like I told you, they'll be planning to rob the outlaws. All we gotta do is make sure the outlaws don't rob us. Go on now, catch up with the Monitor and do like I said.'

McManus did as Casper told him and spurred his horse into a gallop. At last the horsemen looked to be getting near. When they suddenly veered on to the trail of the stage route, Casper became convinced they were the outlaws. A few minutes more and he was able to see that they were. He lay low, waiting for them to pass, and then when they did, he let them ride on further before he swung up on his mount and gave chase under cover of the clouds of dust thrown up by their horses' hooves.

Gene Barnett was meantime cracking a stinging whip over the heads of his team of six. He was not sure that either the horses or the Monitor could take it for long, but he had Casper's orders and he knew Casper's orders were the only thing in this wilderness that could be relied upon to keep himself and the others alive. As they neared the point where the trail dipped sharply, he cracked the whip even harder as he played the reins in an effort to keep the coach more surely under his deft control as it plunged into the thankfully low water of the Cheyenne River.

The closer the Monitor came to the river, the more Blackman and his gang gained upon it. They got to within pistol range and began to fire Colts and Remingtons. Wright, who was riding shotgun, was, thanks to McManus's warning, ready for them, but he was only able to let off half a dozen rounds before his gun jammed. McManus, riding alongside the coach, had better luck and punched a hole straight into Divine's upper jaw. As he fell

he was trampled under the hooves of Casper's
mount.

Casper could see that things were reaching a
critical point and decided it was time he made his
move. As he pulled out a six-gun, he could just see
Blackman through the dust. He took aim and
fired a couple of shots into the rump of his mount.
It stumbled and fell, throwing Blackman clear
and causing the riders close on his tail to swerve
sharply to avoid crashing into the crippled bay.
Ace turned to see who in hell was firing at them
from behind. When he saw that it was Casper, he
knew instantly the game was up and that the best
thing he could do was try and make a getaway.
Reining sharply to the right, he turned his horse
around and galloped off across the prairie. As they
saw him do this, the other members of the gang
split up and rode off in different directions, leaving only Divine's riderless horse racing ahead of
Casper. Ahead of it, the Monitor kept up its pace
as it neared the river.

For some moments Casper fired after the gang
as they fled in all directions, then he pulled up his
mount. As he was taking stock of the situation, he
saw Ace suddenly turn his horse in the direction
of where Blackman's horse had fallen. Blackman

had struggled to his feet and Ace had seen him. It now became a race between Ace and Casper as to who would get to Blackman first. It would have been Casper, had his attention not suddenly been diverted by the screams of the Sioux war party, which had appeared and was in full pursuit of the Monitor.

SIX

'S-h-i-t!' Casper exclaimed out loud. He spurred his horse and rode off in the direction of the war party. He knew they must have seen him and the gang as they fought and reckoned they were now after the stagecoach themselves. He decided he had to reach the Monitor before the Sioux did. Breaking off the trail, he took off east, heading for a bend in the river. Galloping like the wind, he kept the war party on his right. He could hear their war cries and reckoned Barnett and the others would be hearing them, too. No matter how often men in the West heard those cries, they always sent shivers down their spines. It was the thought of the fate that awaited them, if they were to lose the battle.

As he neared the bend in the river, Casper caught sight of the stagecoach as it hurtled along, trailing clouds of dust behind it. Without pausing for thought, he plunged into the waters of the Cheyenne. In this stretch of the river the water was shallow and Casper's horse was able to cross it without losing speed. Barnett, McManus and Wright saw him coming and breathed a collective sigh of relief. Barnett, knowing his team of horses had been running hard for some time, was wondering for how much longer they were going to be able to keep it up. He could see the sweat on their bodies and the foam at their mouths.

'Keep heading for Sage Creek,' Casper called out to him, as he drew up level with the Monitor. 'Maybe we can outrun 'em.'

As he spoke the redskins fired their first shots. Casper swung his horse around to line up with McManus, who had been riding left of the rear of the stagecoach.

'Reckon we oughta try and divert their attention a bit. Ride out in a circle and come up behind them,' he shouted to him.

'OK,' McManus replied, letting off a number of shots from his Remington 1875.

'Wait till I give the word,' Casper said.

The war party was gaining on them fast. They lost two of their number to Wright's brilliant aim with a rifle but this did not deter them. Lead whistled past Barnett and Wright; it was only a matter of time before one of them took a hit.

Casper rode up to the Monitor and shouted out to Barnett informing him of what he was planning to do. He was half-way through telling him when one of the sweetest sounds to be heard by anyone under attack from Indians began to reach their ears. A cavalry bugler was sounding the charge. A patrol was coming from down the trail; it had started out from the way station at Sage Creek where the soldiers had heard the gunfire. Within a matter of minutes they were breaking ranks and riding either side of the Monitor to charge at the Indians, joined by Casper and by McManus who hollered loud cheers of welcome as he rode along.

At first the Indians continued to come on but then, realizing they were hopelessly outnumbered, they took off in full flight across the prairie. Led by a sergeant, half the company of soldiers followed them, while the other half came to a halt, Casper and McManus with them.

'Were we glad to see you,' Casper said to a young lieutenant.

'It looks like we arrived in the nick of time,' the lieutenant remarked.

'You could say that,' McManus said, removing his hat and mopping his brow with a neckerchief.

'We've been looking for that bunch of renegades for days.'

'They ain't the only ones causing trouble in these parts. Just before they attacked we were fending off a gang of road agents a few miles back on the other side of the river,' Casper said. 'We got a couple of them, but most got away.'

'We'll go and investigate. Don't reckon you'll be having any more trouble from Indians,' the lieutenant said.

'You from the East?' Casper asked him.

'Sure am,' he replied.

'Hmm, thought so,' Casper remarked disparagingly. He turned his horse and headed off in the direction of the Monitor. McManus, putting his hat and neckerchief back in place, nodded his appreciation to the lieutenant and spurred his mount to follow Casper.

'Damn fools, they'll never understand the Indians,' Casper said when McManus drew level with him. 'Not until they've killed them all, and then it won't matter.'

'And ain't that the truth of it?' McManus agreed.

'We'd better see what's happened to the Monitor,' Casper said, spurring his horse into a trot.

They rode all the way into Hat Creek station before they found out.

'What a day!' Gene Barnett sighed on seeing him. 'First outlaws and then Indians. Someone must have been keeping a watchful eye over us,' he added, throwing his gaze upwards. 'We weren't gonna hang around out there to find out who though. Felt kind of naked once you and Mac here had ridden off with the soldiers. Thought we'd better ride on in, 'case those road agents showed up again.'

'Very wise,' Casper said. Then turning to the stock-tender, he asked: 'Bill, did the army say they was planning to come back tonight?'

'Nope,' Bill replied, 'but they didn't take their tents, and they left behind plenty of other gear, so I reckon they will be.'

'OK then,' Casper said. 'Reckon we'll just hang out here for the rest of the day. Ain't much of it left anyways,' he added looking up at the sun.

'Yeah,' agreed Wright. 'I feel about as limp as a worn-out fiddle string.'

'Got any whiskey, Bill?'

'Just some home brew. It's rot-gut stuff, though,' the stock-tender replied.

'It'll do,' Casper said. 'And grub?'

'Only the usual, excepting the army's here, of course. Had some fine beef jerky last night.'

'I'm hungry now, Bill. Reckon we all are. See what you can rustle up,' Barnett said.

'Sure thing,' replied Bill. 'I'll just corral these horses.'

'What do you reckon, Will,' Barnett asked Casper, as they both walked in the direction of a water butt. 'D'you think those road agents have given up?'

'I don't know, Gene. Thought I'd killed their leader but he got up on to his feet the same time the war party showed. I would have had him but for that. Maybe he's feeling beat, maybe not.'

'Wonder who he is?' Barnett mused.

'Yeah, I've been wondering that myself. I got pretty close to him, but it weren't anyone familiar-looking to me,' Casper replied.

They arrived at the water butt, where both men stripped down to their waists.

'But,' Casper continued, 'the company's offering good money for him, so if he doesn't try anything before we get to Cheyenne, reckon I'll go looking for him. I'll speak to the sheriff in Cheyenne, see if his face is on any of his Wanted posters.'

Dunc Blackman and what was left of his gang were holed up on a homestead south west of Custer. They'd been heading for their cabin in the hills above Deadwood but Blackman couldn't manage the ride. His spine had taken a hell of a jolt when he hit the ground and it was all he could do to keep his seat. Once he was sure they were not being followed by Casper or the army, he made Ace pull up and he dismounted.

'I can't go on,' he said to Ace. 'We'll have to find somewheres round here to hide out.'

'But where?' asked Ace, who hadn't realized his boss was hurt so badly. He looked around him. It was getting near dusk.

'There must be a homestead or something nearby,' groaned Blackman, who was lying out on his back on the ground. 'Send Jesse off to see. He looks harmless enough. When he finds somewhere tell him to bring back a wagon for me.'

'You hurt that bad?' Ace asked.

'What does it look like?' Blackman snapped.

Ace told Jesse to do what Blackman wanted. An hour or so later he returned with a wagon and another man driving it. The driver had not been given the true facts, but had been told only that someone was hurt bad out on the prairie and needed help. Homesteaders didn't usually need to be asked twice to help anyone in trouble. It wasn't long, however, before the man, whose name was Baylis, realized what he'd let himself in for. He was no stranger to the West and he knew outlaws when he saw them.

'This ain't what it seems, is it?' he said, turning to Jesse.

'Just shut up and do what you're told,' Jesse snarled. He pulled his Colt, cocked it and pointed it in Baylis's direction.

They got Blackman into the wagon and forced Baylis to drive him back to the farm, about five miles away. Baylis said nothing for the whole of the journey. These were three desperate looking men. He knew how unpredictable and savage outlaws could be and he worried for his family.

As they pulled up outside the Baylis farmhouse, Mary Baylis and their two girls came out to greet them. When she saw that one of the men

was pointing a gun at her husband, she knew
something was wrong.

'It's all right,' Baylis said to her. 'They just want
to rest up for a while while one of them recovers
from a fall off his horse. They ain't gonna harm us,
are you?'

'Not if you do what you're told,' Ace replied.
'Now help Jesse here get Dunc in.'

In the cabin and laid out on the Baylis's bed,
Blackman began issuing orders. He said he
wanted some food and a hot bath in that order.
When the girls began to look frightened and to cry
he told Mary Baylis to shut them up or put them
to bed. When Mary Baylis pointed out to him they
were only children, Blackman told them again
that no harm would come to any of them, so long
as they did what they were told.

'Don't try anything stupid, 'cause I ain't averse
to killing,' Ace said by way of emphasis.

Mary Baylis calmed the girls and told them to
go put their dolls to bed.

'You got anything for drawing out bruises?'
Blackman called from his bath which was
concealed behind a screen of hanging cotton sheets.

'I've got some horse liniment, if that's what you
mean,' Mary Baylis replied.

They'd had some pork and beans and, while she was clearing away the dishes, Blackman bathed.

'Reckon that's exactly what I mean,' Blackman replied. 'I'll be out of this bath in a minute. Maybe then you'd be so kind as to bring it to me.'

Mary Baylis felt no inclination to play nursemaid to Blackman. Angry at the way these men had burst in upon their lives, she grabbed the bottle of liniment from a shelf and thumped it down on the table, saying: 'There it is, if you want it.'

Blackman laughed out loud, while Ned Baylis grimaced nearby. Ace had not let him out of his sight and told him to sit where he was and say nothing every time he looked as if he might want to get up.

'Ha!' Blackman laughed out loud. 'I sure do compliment you on your bedside manner, ma'am, don't you boys?'

'I ain't ever played nursemaid to anyone, exceptin' my family and I don't propose to start doing so now,' Mary Baylis said.

'Aw, now don't be like that,' Ace crooned. 'You being so pretty and all.'

Incensed by Ace's lascivious tone Baylis jumped up and went to get between him and his wife. Ace was quick to pull a gun.

'I told you to stay where you was or else,' he snapped, cocking the trigger of his Colt .45 and pushing Baylis back into his chair with his free hand. 'And you,' he said to Mary Baylis, 'will rub that liniment on Dunc's back. 'Cause the sooner he's better the sooner we can get on our way. That's what you want, ain't it?'

The next day Blackman was feeling a lot better, but he reckoned he ought to rest for at least another day. Blackman was smarting not only from the injuries received when he was thrown from his horse, but also from hurt pride. Will Casper had bettered him twice now when the odds were less than evenly stacked against him, and it galled him bad. Life was a bitch, and now he felt as if he was married to one in the form of fate. A rush of indignation caused his body to tense, which set his bruises smarting.

'Damn that son of a bitch!' he exclaimed out loud. 'Damn that son of a bitch!'

Ace was outside sitting on the porch when he heard Blackman's raised voice. Thinking something was wrong, he burst into the cabin with his gun drawn. 'You all right, boss?' he asked as he stepped into the Baylis's bedroom.

'Yeah,' Blackman replied. 'I was just thinking

about Casper and what happened back there when we was trying to rob the stage.'

'Yeah, he's one lucky dude,' Ace remarked. 'But his luck can't hold out for ever. Next time it might not all go his way.'

Blackman thought for a while, then said, 'It's more than just robbing the stage now. It's personal. Maybe I should go looking for him in Cheyenne or Deadwood.'

Revenge may be sweet, Ace thought to himself, but gold was even sweeter, and you could spend it. Not being in the habit of contradicting Blackman, he did not give voice to his thoughts. Instead, he said: 'Ain't much of our stash left, Dunc.'

'Stagecoaches ain't the only things to rob. Maybe it's time we hit a bank,' Blackman replied.

'Yeah, like we used to in Texas,' enthused Ace. 'God damn it, why didn't I think of that?'

Blackman didn't have a reply. Or, rather, he did, but it would only have hurt Ace's feelings. Instead he thought out loud, 'Which one, though?'

'I'll ride out tomorrow and do some investigating,' Ace said. 'Reckon the bank in Custer might be worth looking at.'

'OK,' agreed Blackman, knowing that discreetly sniffing things out was Ace's real talent. 'Go check it out. I'll be fit to ride in a few days. Jesse can take care of things here 'til you get back.'

SEVEN

Later that day Ace made his way north through the Black Hills to Custer. He left before noon and arrived at sunset.

'Beer,' he said to the bartender, having made his first port of call the saloon. He drank it down in one go and immediately asked for another.

Custer was not as crazy a mining town as Deadwood but it had its share of colour and excitement. So much so that the bartender took little notice of the fact that Ace was a stranger in town. Men blew in, they blew out again.

Ace downed a few more beers, then turned and leaned back with his elbows on the bar, looking around him. There was the usual sight of gamblers, drinkers and good time gals. Gambling he didn't do much of, drinking he only did moderately, but whoring was something he could be excessive about. Casting an eye about, he hoped to come across some pretty little thing to satisfy his need. He was not disappointed. There she was, the girl of his dreams, whispering sweet nothings into a cowboy's ear, a cowboy already so drunk, Ace reckoned, he'd barely notice her being taken away from him. He made his way to her, skirting round tables and groups of drunken prospectors loudly accompanying a piano player who was belting out the ever-rousing 'Old Rosin the Beau'.

'You're wasting your time with him,' he whispered into the girl's ear.

Startled she turned to see who it was. 'Says who?' she asked seductively.

'The look of him,' Ace replied, indicating with a tilt of his head the cowboy in his chair who didn't appear to have even noticed his arrival on the scene.

'I think you could be right,' replied the girl, whose name was Cathy. Running a hand down his cheek, she accepted what she knew was Ace's invitation to go with him.

'Don't the piano pounder know anything else?' Ace asked her, as he led her back to the bar.

'He does,' Cathy replied humorously, 'but they'd shoot him if he got bored with it before they did.'

'What can I get you?' he asked.

'A beer,' was Cathy's reply.

This pleased Ace. A good time gal that drank beer was a good time gal indeed. They drank for a while and she played up to him. Then he led her towards a staircase he'd noticed out of the corner of his eye.

'It'll cost you five dollars,' she whispered, as they climbed the stairs.

'Is that all?' Ace teased her. 'Lead the way,' he added, as they stepped on to the landing.

In a room just vacated by another good time gal and her paying customer, Ace spent his fire. Now he'd be ready to explore the town and gauge how takeable the bank was. All that was needed was daybreak. Leaving Cathy to douche and dress, he quit the saloon and got himself a bed for the night in a nearby hotel. He got up when daybreak came and on the way out of the hotel had himself a good breakfast of ham, eggs, beans and coffee.

On Main Street he took stock of all that was relevant to the job in hand. The bank was big and rich looking. Either side of the front door were two large cut-glass windows of the finest quality. Only

wealth could facilitate the bringing of two such
splendid artefacts up into the Black Hills. Inside
the bank was eminently suited to a robber's
needs. The place was so relaxed it seemed being
robbed was the furthest thing from anyone's
mind. A teller worked behind a barely secure
counter and the strongroom was wide open, laying
bare for all the world to see its plentiful deposits.
In the half-hour or more that Ace kept an eye
peeled nobody bothered to close it. The manage-
ment might have thought the token presence of a
security guard made the need to do so unneces-
sary. By noon Ace reckoned he'd seen all he
needed to. After a wholesome lunch, he was on his
way back to the Baylis's farm to tell Blackman the
good news.

Cheyenne people were marvelling at another
demonstration of Will Casper's ability to beat off
robbers and Indians. He tried to shift some of the
glory to Barnett, Wright and McManus but the
people and the newspaper reporters would not let
the emphasis shift. The gold and the money had
arrived intact at its destination and Casper was
the great hero of the moment – again. Booze
flowed in celebration and Cheyenne was full of

sparkle that night. Back at the Baylis's homestead, Dunc Blackman licked his wounds. He
wasn't ready to ride yet but the news Ace had
brought him about the bank in Custer cheered
him a little.

'So you think it'd be a cinch,' he said.

'Easier than anything we did in Texas,' Ace
replied. 'Looking around that bank, you'd have
thought the words bank robbery had never been
uttered by anyone anywhere. I could have done
the job there and then myself.'

'That's if there are no Will Caspers about,'
Blackman remarked, straightening a still-bruised
leg to ease the pain some.

'There ain't, not in Custer that I could see,' Ace
said.

Casper was not a man to delude himself. It had
been luck, not skill that had saved the stagecoach
from being robbed.

'Don,' he said to the sheriff of Cheyenne, 'I'm
going after those sons of bitches, before my luck
begins to run out and theirs to improve.' They
were sitting in the sheriff's office.

'Have you any idea who might be leading this
gang?'

'No, but I did get a glimpse of their leader and thought maybe if I went through your Wanted posters I might find him amongst them.'

'You sure it ain't Persimmon Bill?' the sheriff asked.

'Yeah, I'd know his face and he'd know mine. Besides, he don't usually go for the big ones, just the little ones that he knows he can handle. This gang bears all the hallmarks of robbery on a grand and determined scale.'

'Sure seems like it,' Sheriff Don Carter remarked.

'That's why I thought maybe I'd look at your Wanted posters. See if I can't see his face in one of them.'

'Sure thing,' Carter said. He went to a chest and opened a drawer that was full of them. 'There's a couple of dozen here and there's a few just in from Texas. News of the gold strikes here don't just attract prospectors. Most of the road agents in these parts have come up from the South.'

Casper leafed through the bundle of Wanted posters Carter handed him.

'Yeah,' he mused. 'Time we sent them back home, I reckon. Maybe we could enlist Persimmon Bill's help. Home-grown scum like him don't take too kindly to outsiders coming in and working their patch.'

'Maybe,' Sheriff Carter said with a smile. 'Don't reckon the town'd take too kindly to me pinning a badge on him, though.'

'Can't see Persimmon liking it much either. It'd confuse things for him. He wouldn't know who to shoot first the good guys or the bad guys,' Casper said.

He'd looked at nearly all of the posters Carter had given him and hadn't come across a face that bore any similarity to the man whose horse he'd shot from under him. Until he came to the last poster. He studied it for a moment. "Dunc Blackman", read the name underneath the face printed on it. "Wanted for 25 bank robberies. Reward: $1,000".

'Reckon that's him,' Casper said at last, holding up the poster and showing it to Carter. 'I didn't get a real good look at him but I'd say he's our man.'

'Dunc Blackman,' Carter read. 'That's one of the Texas posters. Twenty-five robberies. That's big time. If'n those Texas Rangers didn't catch him, it ain't gonna be easy for you to, Will.'

Casper thought for a moment. Then he said:

'The Black Hills ain't like the wide open spaces of Texas, Don. You gotta know the lie of the land in these parts. I know these hills like the back of my hand. That makes it about even, I'd say. And we've already killed some of them. There can't be many of his gang left.'

Carter had watched Casper build his reputation and knew that he was probably right. He was going to suggest a posse but knew that it wasn't the way Casper operated. Instead he asked, 'When you aim to get started?'

'Tomorrow,' Casper replied. 'I gotta get me a good mount first.'

'Which way you gonna head?'

'Back up the trail until I pick up their tracks,' Casper replied. 'Company's got an office in Custer. If I ain't having any luck, maybe I'll drop in there. See if they've been active anywheres.'

EIGHT

Casper gave Wright and McManus the option to ride with him or stay with the Monitor as it made its journey back to Deadwood carrying dry stock. They opted to go with him. They were taking care of last minute arrangements in the company's office. Casper had told them that he was pretty certain he'd identified the leader of the gang who'd tried to hold up the Monitor and he was going after him and what was left of his gang. Both messengers said it would give them the greatest of pleasure to take on Blackman when their actions weren't restricted by being tied to a stagecoach.

'Right,' said Casper, 'we'll leave in the morning. I'll meet you in the livery around ten.'

The next morning, having first passed by the company's office to check out of town, Casper walked to the livery stable. As he did so, his eyes darted everywhere, taking in the length and breadth of Main Street. He never let his guard down, least of all on the busy thoroughfares of frontier towns. Out of the corner of his left eye he saw, crossing Main Street and coming towards him, the face of a man he recognized. The man had been arrested on suspicion of being part of a gang that had robbed a stage. He'd escaped, killing a deputy and a few Deadwood citizens who had been caught in crossfire.

Jim Webb, the name of the suspected stage robber, recognized Casper instantly. His first thought was to run but he knew that would be hopeless. Instead he drew his Colt .45 and fired at him. Quick as lightning Casper dived into a doorway and the shot whistled past him, shattering the window of a general store. Suddenly the air was filled with the screams of alarmed and afraid Cheyenne citizenry. Sheriff Carter came running out of his office.

Casper was quick to fire back but was unable to prevent Webb from jumping on a horse. Webb started off up Main Street firing wildly as he

went. One of Casper's bullets hit him in the arm.
Wright and McManus suddenly appeared and,
along with Sheriff Carter, they too began firing at
Webb. One of their bullets brought down his
horse, sending him flying from it. Webb, though,
managed to hold on to his gun and was quickly
back on his feet, again firing wildly in every direction. Then suddenly his gun chamber was empty.
Clicking on an empty gun, his face became full of
fear.

'Hold your fire, men!' Sheriff Carter called out
to Casper and the others, coming out from behind
the cover of a barbershop doorway. 'He ain't going
nowheres now.'

Webb put his hands up in surrender as Carter
walked towards him. Casper, knowing desperate
men didn't give in so easily, kept his eyes fixed
firmly on Webb.

'Don't shoot Sheriff,' Webb called to Carter in
begging tones.

'I ain't gonna shoot you, son,' the sheriff called,
'just as long as you come quietly.'

By now he was almost face to face with Webb.
Feeling that he'd as good as made his arrest
Carter turned to let the citizens cowering on Main
Street know that it was safe. As he did so, Webb

made a grab for his gun. Before he could loose it from Carter's grip a bullet hit him between the eyes. He stood for a moment as if turned to stone, his eyes bulging, taking in as their last picture the sight of Casper's smoking gun.

'Son of a bitch!' Sheriff Carter muttered to himself, as Webb, still holding on tightly in a dead man's grip to his Colt Peacemaker, crumbled in a heap before him. Carter let the gun fall with him.

'His name is Jim Webb,' Casper informed Carter, as he walked up to him. 'He's wanted in Deadwood for robbery. There's a price of a hundred dollars on his head. I'll collect it when I'm next in town.'

'Yeah, yeah, sure thing,' the sheriff replied.

He wanted to thank Casper for saving his life but didn't get the chance. He was already walking back to where McManus and Wright were standing steadying the horses. Carter knew that what he'd done was not strictly legal, but who would be fool enough to try and arrest him for it? Some of the citizens watching him go didn't like his tactics; the others, the majority, were just glad that someone was brave enough to stand up to the kind of low life that was plaguing the decent folk of the West.

Casper himself couldn't have given a damn what anyone thought of his actions. He hated outlaws and reckoned the only good one was a dead one. And he was tough enough to make sure that any outlaw who did cross his path ended up just that, dead.

'Come on,' he said to Wright and McManus, as he took hold of the reins of his horse and swung himself into the saddle, 'let's go get Blackman.'

Blackman was still resting up and having his bruises tended to back at the Baylis's farm. The worst had been on the tail of his spine but he was beginning to feel at last that he'd soon be able to sit a horse again and ride. Three days had gone by, three days too many. Casper had deprived him of what he thought should have been his and it gnawed away at him, making him feel as if his saddle was slipping and there was no cinch to put right.

It was gone midday and when Ace came into the Baylis's bedroom with a plate of black beans and jerky, he said to him, 'Ace, we'll ride tomorrow.'

'Where to?' Ace asked, handing the food to Blackman.

'Custer,' was his reply, 'we're gonna take that bank and then get out of here and head back down south.'

'You feeling up to it?' Ace asked. 'I mean, it ain't as if there's any hurry.'

Blackman wanted to laugh. They had practically no money left, Casper was no doubt looking for them, and Ace felt there was no hurry.

'Ace,' he said. 'For all your brains, sometimes you're as chuckleheaded as a prairie dog. Of course there's a hurry. We ain't got but a few dollars left and I can't see Casper leaving us in peace for much longer.'

'He's one man, Dunc. He can't ride shotgun and ride posse over the territory, too. If he ain't showed his face yet, I don't reckon he's going to,' was Ace's view.

Blackman tucked into his meal. It was so uninteresting, he felt like spitting it out. 'We ride tomorrow,' he said, pushing the food to one side of his mouth. 'Maybe then we'll be able to find something decent to eat.'

'Ain't nothing wrong with that grub pile,' Ace replied.

'No?' sniffed Blackman, throwing his plate aside. 'You eat it then.'

'Already had my fill 'n' more,' Ace replied, reaching for Blackman's left-overs.

'Bring me some coffee and that map of Custer you drew,' Blackman suddenly said. 'We need to go over things again. I just want to ride into town, rob the bank and ride out again. Even if it's gonna be as easy water as you say, we gotta be sure we all know what we're doing.'

Ace did as he was told. He brought the map he had drawn on a piece of paper torn from a note book he'd acquired in Custer and spread it out on the bed in front of Blackman.

'There's gonna be a lot of money in the bank. I heard tell there was two thousand head of cattle being driven up to Cheyenne from Dodge and more than a handful of them's being brought to Custer. The money must already be sitting and waiting in the vaults for them,' Ace informed him. 'So, if you are feeling up to it, the sooner we take it the better.'

'Yeah,' Blackman said. 'As I said, we ride tomorrow.'

Casper and his two sidekicks rode out over the wide prairie to where they'd been attacked by Blackman and his gang. There had been no rain or wind and Casper was able to pick up their trail with ease. They found Blackman's horse, which was now a bloated carcass showing all the signs of having been picked over by vermin. There was a man's dead body that had suffered a similar fate. It stank something terrible and Casper and his men gave it a wide berth, leaving it to the thousands of flies that buzzed around its oozing mess and foul ordure. There was a mess of hoof prints in the place where Ace had picked up Blackman and then there were the clear signs of one horse, heavily laden, heading off north-west.

'It's as I thought,' Casper said to McManus and Wright. 'Blackman was picked up when the Indians attacked. We'll try and track them and see where it leads.'

'What about the Indians?' Wright asked.

'Expect the army's dealt with them,' Casper replied.

'And if they haven't?' McManus queried.

'Well, they ain't likely to be much trouble to us. We ain't got much they'd want,' Casper said.

'Except'n scalps,' McManus remarked, pushing his Stetson off his head and running his fingers through his long hair.

'They've been wanting my scalp for a long time

but they ain't succeeded yet. Reckon they've maybe given up trying,' Casper said.

Looking over his buckskin suit, McManus thought how he'd always supposed Casper, with his legendary tracking and fighting skills, was as much Indian as he was white man. People said this was why he was so ruthless in dealing with outlaws. Indians showed no mercy, gave no quarter; Casper didn't either.

'Well,' McManus said after a few seconds, 'no doubt the army's keeping them occupied.'

Casper had no time for Indians who strayed from their reservations but equally he hated the way the army slaughtered Indian women, children and old folk in their undefended tepee villages and in so doing sent back word to Washington claiming great victories for themselves in the Indian Wars. It was why he particularly loathed General Custer, reckoning he and his 7th Cavalry had got their come-uppance at the Battle of the Little Big Horn for all the evil they'd done. 'Come on,' he said to the two men, spurring his horse into a trot in the direction Ace and Blackman had taken.

As Casper and McManus, were talking, the platoon of soldiers that had seen off the war party of Indians chasing the Monitor was riding out of Hat Creek station in Sage Creek, Wyoming. They'd been outrun by the war party as it fled but were counting on coming across it somewhere out on the prairie. Reports had come in of attacks on homesteaders and they were riding south-east to investigate. White women and children had been killed. This was a crime more heinous than any imagined on God's earth and something was going to be done about it.

They rode long and hard into the day, checking out each homestead they passed. What they found at some filled them with horror, most others they discovered to be safe and unharmed.

'Their attacks seem to me to be pretty random,' the young lieutenant leading the platoon remarked to one farmer whose homestead had escaped attack so far.

'There ain't no more than a handful of them,' Henry Gladstone, the farmer, replied. 'It's just a wild bunch of young Sioux braves.'

'They've done a lot of harm,' the lieutenant said. 'And they don't show any signs of letting up.'

'You aiming to hang around and wait for them to show up here or what?' Gladstone asked. His wife was indoors and his three young children were standing nearby staring at the soldiers.

'We could maybe camp here for the night, that's if you have no objections, sir. It'll soon be dark and we've got to camp somewhere,' the lieutenant replied.

Gladstone said they'd be welcome and the platoon's sergeant ordered his men to dismount. The children showed great interest in the men as they set up camp. Those soldiers with children of their own enjoyed their company immensely and let the children go where their curiosity led them. The lieutenant ate with Gladstone and his wife and Gladstone regaled him with tales of life on the frontier. The lieutenant told his tale of preventing a stagecoach robbery and seeing off a band of Indian renegades at the same time and a pleasant evening was had by all. It was with some heaviness of heart that the soldiers and the Gladstones parted company the next morning.

'Won't you stay another night?' the lieutenant was asked.

'It's very kind of you, sir,' the lieutenant replied, 'but we have our work to do and I'd hate to think we were putting people's lives at risk by not doing it.'

'I sure hope you don't find any more homesteads have been attacked by them red-skinned savages,' Mrs Gladstone declared. 'We've been lucky so far, but I don't know how long a person's luck can hold out in these here wilderness parts.'

Later that morning the Baylis's found out that sometimes luck can desert you altogether. For as Blackman rode off the Indians rode in. He and the remains of his gang were still close enough to have heard the war cries of the Indians. They decided, however, it was none of their business and continued on their way.

Baylis was in the fields trying to round up the cattle and sheep that Blackman's presence had forced him to neglect, while his wife was in the garden hanging sheets out to dry which she reckoned Blackman had defiled and which she had scrubbed until her fingers were almost raw. The children were playing close by. Mary Baylis heard the Indians first. They came from out of nowhere, charging across the fields, scattering the livestock with their piercing war cries.

'Oh my God!' she exclaimed out loud, turning to look for the children. 'Not this. Not now, not after what we have just been through.'

Then everything happened very quickly. Baylis

came running, a Winchester rifle in hand. He saw his wife reach the children and pull them close in around her. As he fired at the Indians, they charged at his family, riding into them with their horses and trampling them as they fell. None of his bullets hit home and soon he ran out. He himself took a bullet in the chest and the last thing he saw as he fell to the ground dying was his wife being set upon by the Indians. They stripped her naked and did unspeakable things to her as the children in a dazed and shocked state looked on.

The Indians took it in turns to rape her. One, who'd been first in line, drew a long knife. He ran and scalped her dead husband and then, as the blood lust began to rage in him even more fiercely than the sex lust, he hurried back to where Mary Baylis was enduring her last rape. As she began to fall into unconsciousness, he waited in readiness to cut off her breasts. The other Indians, their lust all spent, were about to turn their attentions to the slaughter of the children when they were suddenly brought to their senses by the sound of gunfire and bullets whistling about their heads. Casper, Wright and McManus were racing across the fields towards them. Quick as lightning the Indians grabbed their weapons, mounted their horses and galloped away. They hadn't gone far when they saw the army platoon heading straight towards them at full tilt. Veering off to the left, they tried to escape but found themselves caught in a storm of lead that cut through them from the army on one side and Casper, Wright and McManus on the other. To a man, they all fell. A few died instantly, while the rest lay wounded in the grass where they'd fallen. It was Casper who rode in amongst them and finished them off one after another.

The army rode on to the Baylis's farm. The sight that greeted them made some of them want to puke and others actually to do so. The sergeant jumped off his horse and ran to the children, who were still standing huddled together, too shocked and frightened to move, while the young lieutenant ran to their mother. She was still alive. His first thought was to cover her nakedness. Looking around him he saw a large white sheet hanging on the clothesline. He ran and snatched it and then hurried back to cover her with it.

'It's all right, ma'am, it's all right,' he said as he tucked it around her, 'we're here now. They're all dead. We're here.'

'My babies?' she asked through cut and swollen lips.

'They're here, they're all right,' the lieutenant told her.

'And my husband?' she asked.

Before the lieutenant had a chance to answer her, a corporal whose job it was to act as doctor to the platoon said he thought they should carry her into the house. She asked again about her husband. The lieutenant looked to the corporal for a lead in what to say.

'I'm sorry, ma'am, but I'm afraid he's dead,' the corporal said.

Mary Baylis was barely strong enough to react and she lapsed into unconsciousness.

'Come on,' the corporal said, turning to a soldier standing nearby, 'help me get her inside.'

The lieutenant walked over to where the sergeant was standing with his arms around the children.

'Your mother's going to be all right,' he said to them in comforting tones. To Sergeant Jones he said, 'Better take them inside.' Then he turned and began to walk to where the body of their father lay. Already flies were buzzing around the bloody mess of his head. 'Soldier,' he said quietly to a man close by, 'get a spade and someone to help you bury him.'

NINE

Casper and his men stayed on at the Baylis's farm. The army stayed, too, but on the morning of the third day the lieutenant said they would have to leave to continue their patrol. There were probably more Indians about and he thought they ought to go and check on other farms in the area.

'I don't think we can leave Mrs Baylis and the children here alone. And a doctor ought to look at her,' he advised Casper.

'I was thinking of stopping off at Custer. Maybe I should take her and the children with me. She'll find a doctor there,' Casper said. 'I'll put it to her.'

When told by Casper what his plans were, Mary Baylis tried to tell him about Blackman and his plans to rob the bank at Custer, but she was

too weak to be able to say it. Casper put her
attempts at trying to say something down to anxi-
ety at leaving the farm. He tried to reassure her
everything would be OK, that she could return
when she was ready. Then when she said no more,
he assumed she was reassured. They turned the
livestock loose to graze at will on the prairie and
Wright drove the Baylis family in the covered
wagon in which they had come to Dakota
Territory eight years before. Casper rode his
mount alongside. His mind was filled with bitter
thoughts about all the vermin in this world that
use and abuse innocent folk like the Baylises. He
wanted to kill them all. At least they'd done for
that band of savages. His thoughts then turned to
Dunc Blackman and his gang, the real job in
hand. They could be anywhere in the territory but
he was determined he was going to hunt them
down and mete out to them the kind of treatment
they deserved.

In fact Blackman and his gang were biding their
time in a wood close to Custer, getting ready to
rob the bank. The ride from the Baylis farm had
taken it out of Blackman and he'd decided to wait
a day or two to recover before riding into Custer.

He'd sent Jesse to the gang's hideout above Deadwood to get the others and he'd sent Ace back into Custer to double check on things and to make sure the thorn in their side, Will Casper, was not there.

That Casper was not there, Ace had made himself quite certain. Everything looked to him as it had before. Robbing the bank was going to be easy; he saw nothing to make him change his mind about that. After a night in town he decided to ride back to the gang's hideout to tell Blackman. Little did he know that as he rode east out of town, Casper and the covered wagon rode in from the west.

Mary Baylis had shown no signs of recovery as they'd crossed the prairie.

'Reckon we'd better take Mrs Baylis straight to a doctor,' Casper said to Wright, who was driving the covered wagon, as they hit town.

'Sure thing,' Wright replied.

It was near noon and the town was full of activity, with people and horse-drawn vehicles filling Main Street. They soon found a doctor's consulting rooms and Mrs Baylis was carried in. The children remained in the wagon.

'Goodness, what's happened here?' the doctor, whose name was Reid, exclaimed when he saw her.

'Indian attack,' Casper replied. 'They killed her husband and raped her. There's children in the wagon outside. They're unharmed, except for what they saw, of course.'

'Right,' said Doctor Reid. 'Bring her through here. He led them into a backroom. His wife, a nurse, rushed to help. Wright and McManus, who were carrying Mary Baylis, did as they were told and gently put her down on the doctor's couch.

'We'll leave you to it,' Casper said, indicating to Wright and McManus that they should leave.

'Is there anyone to take care of the children?' the doctor's wife asked.

'No,' replied Casper. 'We ain't got much out of Mrs Baylis or the children since the attack. There might be someone in town they could go to, but we don't know.'

'All right.' Mrs Reid followed Casper out of the backroom. 'Bring the children in and I'll see to them.'

She already had in mind someone in town who would be only too ready to take the children in and look after them.

'Thank you, ma'am,' replied Casper. 'We'd be mighty grateful. Those poor children need taking care of, after what they've been through. I'll stop by later and see how Mrs Baylis is.'

'Are you connected with these people in any way, Mr . . . er?' the doctor's wife asked of Casper.

'Casper,' he said. 'Will Casper. No we're not. We came across them when they were under attack. The army was there too. We could see Mrs Baylis was in need of some doctoring and decided to bring her into town. Didn't see how we could leave her and the children there anyways.'

'Were there many Indians?' Mrs Reid asked, taking the children from Wright and McManus, who had tenderly lifted them from the back of the wagon and put them down on the boardwalk in front of her.

'A small war party. We got 'em all though,' Casper replied.

Mrs Reid didn't enquire any more. Instead she led the children into the consultation rooms.

'Goodbye, y'all,' McManus said to the children, as they were led away, 'and take care.'

The children turned and stared but made no reply, the trauma of it all still very much with them.

'Come on now,' Mrs Reid said to them, 'we'll find somewhere nice for you to stay.'

'Take the wagon and the horses to the livery stable,' Casper instructed Wright and McManus. 'I'll go see the agent and meet you in that saloon over yonder later.'

'Sure could do with a drink,' McManus remarked, looking at Wright.

'Yeah,' agreed Wright. 'Drink first, bath later.'

Casper smiled and left the men. He could have done with a drink himself, but first he wanted to find out if anything had been heard of Dunc Blackman and his gang. He was familiar with Custer and was soon stepping into the agent's office. The agent didn't know Casper by face but once Casper introduced himself he knew who he was right away.

'Well, it sure is nice to meet you, Mr Casper, but what brings you to Custer? Ain't this off your patch some?' the agent asked.

Casper told him what his business was and soon ascertained from the agent, a timid, if efficient-looking man, that nothing had been heard in these parts of Blackman and his gang.

'Last thing I heard was that someone had tried to hold up the Monitor when you was riding messenger. If that's who this Blackman is, I don't know no more than that.'

Casper thanked the man and took his leave of him, saying he'd be in town a day or two and then he'd be off hunting road agents again.

'Well, drop in before you leave,' the agent said.

'I'll try,' Casper replied, though feeling there'd be little point. Custer's importance as a gold-mining town wasn't what it used to be and the company was in many ways beginning to pass it by. More worthwhile, he thought, would be a visit to the town marshal.

'Will,' Sheriff Mailer greeted Casper on seeing him come through his office door. 'Why, this is a surprise!'

Casper and Mailer went back a long way to when they first met up on the trail from Wyoming to the Black Hills. Like Casper, Mailer had not taken to prospecting, finding himself more inclined to get involved with the making of a town than chasing a rainbow in the hope it would lead to a fortune. He'd spent a year or more as a deputy before being made sheriff. He'd made a success of the job and the town on the whole was fairly peaceable.

'Hi, Tom,' Casper replied, shaking Mailer's strong right hand.

They exchanged politenesses before Mailer got to hear of the tragedy that had brought Casper to town.

'That's bad, Will. Them Indians have been causing trouble all round these parts for a few weeks now.'

'Well, that particular bunch won't be causing no more trouble,' Casper remarked, pulling up a chair and sitting opposite Mailer who was sitting at his desk.

'Does that mean you got them all?' Mailer asked.

'Yep, every last one of them,' Casper replied, a satisfying picture of the Indians lying dead and wounded on the Baylis's farm filling his mind. Made sure of that myself.'

'Good, good,' remarked Mailer. 'I know there are good Indians, but for the most part the best Indian is a dead'n.' Casper showed he agreed by the look in his eyes. 'That poor woman,' Mailer added.

'Yeah,' Casper agreed solemnly.

There was a silence while the two men quietly reflected on Mary Baylis's pitiful plight. Then Mailer asked, 'Have some coffee, Will?' Casper said he would. 'Heard you ran into some trouble of

your own taking the Monitor down to Cheyenne?'
Mailer remarked, filling a tin mug with coffee
from a pot on a stove and handing it to Casper.

'Yeah,' Casper replied. 'It seems there's a new
road agent operating in these parts. Saw a
Wanted poster in Cheyenne with a picture of a
man called Dunc Blackman on it. I got close
enough to the leader of the gang that tried to rob
the stage and I'd say it was him. He was thrown
from his horse during the chase but before I could
get to him a party of Sioux got between us and we
had to make a run for it. Lucky for us and for him
the army showed up. Got the poster here.'

He pulled it out from a pocket inside his buckskin jacket and handed it to Sheriff Mailer.

'Looks a mean son of a gun,' Mailer remarked,
looking at the picture of a dark, heavily mous-
tached, square-jawed face sitting beneath a flat-
topped 'Boss of the Plains' Stetson.

'Ain't seen him in town, have you?' Casper
asked.

'No,' replied Sheriff Mailer, 'we get our fair
share of long riders here but I ain't seen a one
resembling him. I'll keep a look out though.'

He handed the Wanted poster back to Casper,
who folded it up and put it back in his pocket. 'You

ain't heard if he or anyone's struck again on any of the company's routes?'

'Can't say I have,' Mailer replied. 'Not since you was hit, anyway. You planning to stay in town for long, Will?'

'For a night or maybe two,' Casper replied, getting up. 'I'll be staying at the Golden Nugget. Come along later and I'll buy you a drink. We can talk over old times.'

'I'd like that, Will!' Sheriff Mailer replied. 'I really would!'

Walking out of the sheriff's office on to Main Street, Casper took a long look up and down town. He didn't reckon Blackman would be stupid enough to go into any town in the Dakota Territory but then again he knew most outlaws knew no other way than recklessly to live their generally short lives. There was a number of people going about their business but none, however, that bore any resemblance to Dunc Blackman. Before venturing across Main Street to the Golden Nugget Casper thought he'd go check on Mrs Baylis. It was an hour since he'd dropped her off at the doctor's and he'd be bound by now to have an opinion on her condition.

He found the doctor in his consulting rooms looking very worried.

'I'm afraid she's in a very bad way, Mr . . . er . . . um . . .' the doctor said.

'Casper, Will Casper,' Casper informed him.

'There's a lot of internal damage and I don't know if she'll make it. The next few weeks will tell. She'll have to stay here and be nursed.'

Embarrassed by the talk of intimacies regarding Mrs Baylis's condition, Casper very quickly moved the discussion on.

'Will her children be taken care of, Doctor?' he asked.

'Oh yes, my wife has taken care of that. The preacher's wife is barren and will only be too pleased to take the children in for as long as is necessary.'

'Good,' Casper said. 'Is Mrs Baylis up to having visitors?'

'I don't think so at the moment,' Doctor Reid replied. 'She is heavily sedated and will remain so for some days.'

'Right, well, I'll leave her in your hands. What about the cost?'

'We don't need to worry about that. The town has a fund for victims of Indian attacks, which I am sure will provide amply for Mrs Baylis and her children.'

'I always said this was a good town,' Casper remarked. 'Well, perhaps you will tell Mrs Baylis when she's well enough that I will be coming by before long to see how she is. If she's worried about the farm, tell her not to be, that I will keep an eye on it.'

'Yes, I will,' the doctor said. 'The news will comfort her greatly, I'm sure. I know the family well and know how hard both she and her husband worked on that land of theirs. It is a terrible tragedy that all this has happened. Baylis was a good man and a devoted husband but Mrs Baylis is a strong woman, too, and if she survives, will, I'm sure, want to pick up the pieces of her family's life and carry on.'

Reassured, though still fiercely angry about what had happened to the Baylis family, Casper took his leave of the doctor and made his way to the Golden Nugget. In the bar he found McManus and Wright. Both men had downed a number of beers and were sitting with pretty women on their laps. Casper nodded an acknowledgement to them and went to the bar to order a drink. He looked about him to see where the most inviting looking game of poker was going on. It was barely late afternoon, but the Golden Nugget was already humming with life. Knocking back a first shot of red-eye, Casper suddenly felt himself relaxing. It was only in saloons and hotel bars that he was able to forget for a time what he felt his mission in life to be. Being a man who worked hard at that mission, it was lucky he was also the sort who knew how to play hard. He had a few hundred dollars in his pocket and he was either going to build on it or lose it. Which ever it was, didn't bother him particularly, so long as the game was good. He decided to join the table around which a beautiful belle, whom he assumed to be the madam, was hovering.

Sitting in on the game was a legendary card player who was a half-caste Sioux known as Stabber, so called because of his prowess with a hunting knife. He was dressed, as always, as a dandy, sporting a richly coloured waistcoat. It was said his father had been a great rancher in Texas and his mother the daughter of a great Indian chief, but nobody knew for certain. Stabber himself never commented on the rumours, making them all the more sensational. Whatever his background, wherever he came from, he had won the respect of every white man in Dakota Territory for his skill at the card table, a rare enough feat for anyone, let alone an Indian half caste.

He and Casper had met before at poker and usually Stabber came off the best. Casper was not someone to be prejudiced against anyone because of his race, but this day, after the Indian savagery he had witnessed out at the Baylis farm, his feeling for Indian ways was being sorely tested. Consequently, he had decided that this time he was going to clean Stabber out and give all the proceeds to the Baylis widow. He left the bar and made his way between the tables and revellers on the floor to where Stabber and two other men were completing playing a hand. Stabber had won.

'Mind if I join you?' Casper asked as he approached the table.

'Will!' Stabber exclaimed on seeing who it was. 'Sure thing. Come and join us. Gentlemen, I want to introduce you to a great card-player, not to mention hunter, tracker and above all fighter, Will Casper.' As he pulled up a chair, Casper and the other two men exchanged greetings. They were playing five-card stud.

'Will Casper,' the beautiful hostess, whose name was Lilly, remarked. 'I've heard of you but never had the pleasure.'

She held out a slim, beautiful hand, which Casper gently shook.

'Pleasure's all mine, ma'am.'

'Good, good!' Stabber exclaimed effusively. 'Now, let's get on with the game.'

The other two players were introduced as Casper took a place opposite Stabber, who dealt. His first hand was not bad but he threw it in before the betting got too high and the man on his left won it, not with great cards but because he raised the stakes high. The next hand was won by Stabber.

'That's me out,' said the man to Casper's right. They'd been playing for some time and for him luck had not been a lady that afternoon.

In the next hand that was played Stabber dealt Casper a bad hand. He changed all his cards and found himself with a running flush of five hearts. He had $170 left. Stabber had four times as much as that piled high in front of him. The pot was five each and Casper wanted at the very least to double his money. He could see that Stabber was studying him but he knew he was giving nothing

away. Roy Cole, the man to his right, raised the
bet by five dollars.

'I'll raise you twenty,' Casper said, throwing in
a couple of bills.

Stabber raised the betting another twenty. Cole
threw in his hand.

A bottle of whiskey sat on the table. Casper
didn't know whose it was but he pointed at it as if
to ask if he might and Stabber told him to help
himself. Lilly, who was still hovering, came to a
halt beside Stabber and smiled over at Casper.
He, though, didn't look up from his cards and her
smile went unanswered.

'Raise you fifty,' Stabber said.

This time Casper did look up. Stabber's
demeanour gave away nothing. It had been said in
the past that he cheated but he'd never been
caught and Casper had concluded it was the kind
of sour grapes spouted by his victims. He decided
he'd give him the benefit of the doubt until expe-
rience proved otherwise.

'OK,' he said at last. 'And I'll see you fifty.'

Despite the noise all around them the tension
around the table began to heighten. It was
Stabber's call. Casper looked at his hand. Six,
seven, eight, nine, ten. Could Stabber's hand be

better, he asked himself. Stabber poured himself a shot of whiskey and knocked it back.

'I'll see you and raise you another fifty,' he said at last.

Casper decided he'd show his hand. Indicating thus, he spread his cards out on the table. Stabber's three eights did not beat them and what Casper pulled towards him more or less achieved his intention to double his money. Stabber simply smiled as he collected up the cards and got them ready to deal again. Casper won that hand and the next two. Stabber's losses began to mount. By this time Cole was no longer playing, leaving just Stabber and Casper in the game. The pile of green backs and silver dollars that Casper had in front of him was now higher than that of Stabber's.

'You're cleaning me out,' Stabber jokingly remarked.

'Yeah, well,' commented Casper out loud, while thinking to himself there was a price to be paid by Stabber's people and today it was going to be Stabber that paid it.

Stabber dealt again. This time he won. The next hand he lost and the hand after that gave Casper a royal flush. It was a hand that turned out to be worth more than two thousand dollars.

Lilly had begun by now to make sure he could not miss her smiles. The bottle of whiskey on the table was practically empty, nearly all of it having been drunk by Casper. But he was a big man who had always been able to hold his drink. Lilly called to the bar for another bottle to be brought over. One of her better beauties did the honours, running a hand over Casper's shoulders as she leant over him to put the bottle down and take away the empty one.

'It's on the house,' Lilly declared over the raucus din of the saturated revellers.

'Lilly is nothing, if not generous,' remarked Stabber, who had been dealing. He laughed and made great play with his hands as he dealt but their movement did not hide from Casper the sleight of hand that introduced into the game a different pack of cards which had not been newly shuffled.

'I saw that,' he said.

'Saw what?' Stabber asked.

'That's a new pack of cards and you haven't shuffled them.'

'You calling me a cheat?' Stabber asked, coolly looking Casper in the eye.

'Yeah,' Casper replied.

'Gentlemen, gentlemen,' Lilly said, trying to calm things between them.

Casper thought she was probably in on it by the way she'd hung around the table but he did not say so.

'You can't deny that's a new pack you're dealing from,' he said instead to Stabber.

'I can and I do,' Stabber replied, sure he could bluff his way out of it.

'Let's look at the cards then,' Casper said.

Stabber knew that if they did that it would soon become apparent they were marked. 'I resent the insinuation that I'm a cheat and will not carry on this game,' he said, standing up.

'I've heard it said you're a cheat but I never believed it,' Casper said.

The people around them had suddenly gone silent and Stabber knew that he was in a danger-ous situation. He had to continue to bluff it out or – throw a knife. Lilly came to his rescue.

'Mr Casper, Stabber has gambled at cards here a mighty long time and nobody before has accused him of cheating,' she said.

'That's as maybe, but I know he changed the pack of cards. Let's see what's in his hand,' was Casper's reply.

Stabber knew now that the game was up, for in his hand was a royal flush. A fact that all concerned would reckon to be more than a coincidence. He was wearing a pair of ivory-handled silver Colts, but these were only a ruse to detract from his preferred means of defence. They fooled no one around this gambling table though. He was too well known to them all. Suddenly standing up and overturning the table, he pretended to go for the Colts while in fact producing a throwing knife seemingly from nowhere. But before he could make use of it, Casper drew and shot him.

The fact that Stabber had gone for a weapon first confirmed to everyone that he was a cheat and when Casper left the bar that evening it was with enough winnings to keep the Baylis widow and her children for a long time to come.

TEN

Dunc Blackman planned to ride into town and take the bank at eleven the next morning. He felt he'd rested up enough and was itching to get on with the job. Casper, on the other hand, toyed with the idea of leaving first thing but then decided he should wait and put his winnings in the bank, either in the Baylis account, if they had one, or else in a new account for the widow. He was fairly tight by the time he hit the sack and he woke in the morning with a heavy head. Lilly had tried to charm him but he was not convinced she'd had no part in Stabber's cheating ways and he gave her the cold shoulder, while choosing another whore with whom to sport. Wright and McManus had no reason to doubt their whores and had a fine old time with them. Nursing sore heads, they were glad with what Casper declared.

'Got some business to do in town, boys,' Casper said, having breakfasted. 'Be ready to leave first light tomorrow.'

'Sure thing, boss,' Wright said, fork in hand, playing about with some scrambled eggs and hash browns on a plate in front of him. He didn't feel much like eating.

'Yeah, OK,' McManus agreed.

Casper stepped out of the Golden Nugget into a fine summer's morning. Unlike Wright, what he wanted first thing in the morning after a heavy night before was a big breakfast featuring strong black coffee. Once he'd had it his head became as clear as if he'd spent the night in holy sobriety.

As he crossed Main Street. with all its hustle and bustle, he remembered the events of the night before. In his breast pocket was a bundle of greenbacks. Patting it, he decided he'd make his first port of call the doctor's to see how the widow was. He was just in time to catch Dr Reid, climbing aboard his buggy.

'Morning, Doctor,' he said in greeting.

'Morning, Mr Casper.'

'How's the patient doing?' Casper asked.

'Well, I think there's some cause for hope. She had a good night and this morning was asking after her children,' Doctor Reid informed him.

'Reckon she's up to seeing a visitor?' Casper asked.

'Well, she's sedated again. My wife's in there. Better ask her,' the doctor replied. 'I've got a mess of people to look in on.'

'I'll do that. Thank you, doctor,' Casper replied, standing back to let him get on his way. Then he mounted the boardwalk and stepped into the doctor's consulting rooms.

'Why, good morning, Mr Casper,' Mrs Reid smiled on seeing him.

Greeting her, he told her of his conversation with her husband and asked if she thought Mrs Baylis was in any shape for a visit from him.

'I think she might be pleased to see you,' she replied, 'but don't expect too much. She'll be able to hear you but probably won't be up to talking much. She's still very weak.

'Does she remember much?' Casper asked.

'I think so. She cried when she talked of her husband but was relieved to know the children were being taken care of. I told her you said you'd keep an eye on the farm. I thought she tried to say

117

something else, but as she spoke she lapsed into unconsciousness and I didn't get it.'

'Do you reckon I should call back later?' Casper asked.

'No, that was some time ago. I think she may be awake now,' the doctor's wife replied.

She let him into the room in which Mary Baylis was sleeping. Looking at her, with her face so pale and her mouth and neck still bruised, Casper felt all the anger he'd experienced over the Indian attack come rushing back. It satisfied him greatly to think of what had happened the night before. Bending down over her, he whispered into an ear.

'Mrs Baylis, I'm the man who brought you into town. I just want you to know that everything's going to be all right. I made you a lot of money last night and it will be in the bank waiting for you when you're well enough to go get it. You ain't got nothing to worry about, just getting well for your children.'

Casper noticed that what he'd said seemed to agitate rather than console her. Remembering that his breath would be pretty foul after all the drinking the night before, he moved away from her. He was not the sort to feel romantic where women were concerned, but somehow he felt a rush of tenderness for this woman lying in her bed of loss and sorrow. He'd had little to do with women other than whores in hotels and saloons and there they'd never seemed to him to be help- less and at risk. But a woman helping her husband carve a home out of a wilderness, that was something different. She didn't deserve what had happened to her and he wished he could somehow turn back the hands of time and put it all right for her.

As he looked down at her she seemed to become more agitated. Thinking it was due to his pres- ence being a reminder of what had happened to her, Casper decided he'd best leave right away. He did not hear Mary mumble as he turned and left the room that the bank was going to be robbed.

'Thank you, ma'am,' he said to the doctor's wife. 'She's a long way off being right, I can see, and I'm glad she's in good hands.'

'Well, she'll sleep all morning now,' the doctor's wife said in reassuring tones. Thanking her again, Casper took his leave, noticing as he went a clock on the wall that said it was a few minutes after 9.30. The bank would be open but he decided that before going to deposit his previous night's winnings he'd look in on Sheriff Mailer, whose

office was only a short walk from the doctor's. The
sheriff had been called to the Golden Nugget after
the shooting the night before but he could see at a
glance what had happened and apart from order-
ing Stabber's body to be taken away, he'd taken no
action. He was standing over a stove pouring
himself a mug of coffee when Casper stepped into
his office. Greeting him cheerily he offered him a
mug.

'Yeah, I ain't had enough of that this morning,'
joked Casper.

Smiling, Mailer sat down at his desk and
Casper took a seat opposite him.

'I just been to see the Baylis widow,' Casper
remarked.

'Good or bad?' Mailer asked.

'Good, I reckon. Doctor seems to think so,
though she's obviously got a long way to go,'
Casper replied.

'What are your plans?' Mailer asked.

'Go find Blackman and his gang. We'll leave
first light tomorrow.'

'The stage is due in day after.'

'Yeah, well, ain't got time to wait that long,'
Casper replied.

'Maybe you ought to make time. They might

know if the gang's been active since you last had dealings with them,' Mailer replied. He opened a drawer of his desk, pulled out some tobacco makings, and offered them to Casper.

'Yeah, they might,' Casper agreed, 'but they probably won't have. The stage won't be carrying anything worth robbing.' He wasn't a regular smoker but he nevertheless made himself a roll-up and then handed back the makings to Mailer. While they were smoking and talking the undertaker's wagon came down Main Street, carrying the coffin of Stabber.

'There goes another to Boot Hill,' the sheriff remarked.

'Ever heard before that he cheated?' Casper asked, throwing a glance in the direction of the undertaker's wagon as it passed by.

'He came out on top so often that people wondered but no one ever caught him at it before,' Mailer replied.

'Rare that a half-breed climbs so high in society.'

'The white half of him was already so high born that people hardly noticed the red skin in him,' the sheriff said.

'Yeah, well that was all I saw in him once I saw

121

him switch packs,' Casper remarked. 'It gave me some satisfaction that he went for a knife. I've decided to give all my winnings to the Baylis widow. Reckon that way the Indians are making some recompense for what they did to her and her family.'

'That's pretty noble, Will,' Sheriff Mailer said. 'A lot of folks would be mighty impressed with that.'

'Yeah, well, I don't want it advertised,' Casper stated firmly. 'I'm just telling you so that you'll know and can tell her in case she didn't hear me just now when I told her. If she pulls through, you can comfort her with the fact. If she doesn't, it'll be something for her orphan children.'

'As I say, Will, it's a fine gesture.'

'Well, as I said, it came from a thievin' Indian. There has to be some justice in this life.'

As Sheriff Mailer and Casper were talking about Casper's fine gesture, Dunc Blackman and his gang were riding the last few miles from their hideout to Custer. There were six of them, including Blackman, and all were wearing Tower's Pommel Slickers. They had brought them up from Texas, where they were commonly worn by cowpunchers. Blackman had always dressed his gangs in them when going into action against banks. He reckoned a uniform look gave them the air of an irresistible force that would overawe anyone who got in their way, inside or outside the bank. He rode on now, mean, menacing and without looking back.

'Well, Tom,' Casper said, noticing from a clock on the sheriff's wall that time was passing, 'reckon I'll get over to the bank and deposit that money. Then I aim to have me a long bath and a general clean-up in the barber's shop.'

'OK,' said Mailer, 'I've got a lot to do myself Don't know where that deputy of mine is. He should have been here an hour ago. See you later, Will?'

'Yeah, and we'll have that drink tonight. Talk over old times.'

'Sure thing.' With that Casper left Sheriff Mailer's office and crossed the street to the bank.

The bank in Custer had never been robbed and there was only one man sitting outside it as security. He wasn't exactly formidable looking, even if he did have an old carbine sitting on his lap. He was sleeping as Casper stepped on to the boardwalk in front of the bank and went up the steps to go inside. A fine-looking lady was making her exit.

'Morning, ma'am,' Casper said, raising his hat and stepping back to let her pass. She smiled graciously in acknowledgement. Inside he stepped up to the counter and addressed the teller standing there.

'Can you tell me if the Baylis family have an account here?' he asked.

'Good morning, sir,' the teller politely greeted him. 'Do you mean the family that was attacked by Indians?'

'Indeed I do,' Casper replied.

'A very sad business indeed. I do believe Mary Baylis is being looked after by the doctor's good wife,' the clerk remarked.

'That is correct,' Casper said. 'Now I asked you if the family have an account here?'

'That, sir, I am afraid I am not at liberty to divulge to you.'

'And if I wanted to deposit a sum of money for them?' Casper asked, becoming somewhat impatient. He hated bureaucracy, knowing how it generally failed the people it purported to serve.

'You would have to know the number of their account if indeed they had one here,' the teller replied, puffing himself up to look important.

'Well, perhaps I'd better talk to the manager,' Casper said.

The manager was in fact sitting at a desk not far removed from the counter at the back of the bank. He had heard Casper's enquiry and had been interested to know how the teller would respond to it. Pleased that the man was playing it by the book, he had waited patiently to be asked to intervene in the interests of compassion and common sense.

He got up from his desk, stepped forward, and asked Casper if he might not like to come into his office. Casper accepted the invitation and sat in a chair offered to him by the bank manager.

As he drew the money he intended to deposit in the Baylis family account, Blackman and his gang began to trot down Main Street in the direction of the bank. Some people eyed them with suspicion but most people were too busy going about their business to notice them. Two of the people who did notice them, however, were Wright and McManus, both of whom had just then stepped out of the Golden Nugget to take the air.

'I hope you'll forgive our teller, Mr . . . er . . . um . . .' the manager began.

'Casper, William D. Casper,' Casper informed him.

'Thank you, Mr Casper,' continued the manager, 'but we do have our procedures to adhere to and our tellers cannot be too careful.'

'I'm sure,' Casper replied. 'Now can we please get on with depositing this money?'

'Yes, yes, of course,' the manager replied. He called to the clerk to bring him a paying-in slip.

As the clerk turned and stepped into the manager's office, Dunc Blackman and four of his gang strode into the bank, unnoticed by the guard outside who was snoring heavily.

'This is a hold up,' Dunc Blackman shouted. 'Put your hands up and no one will get hurt!'

The hands of the startled teller, who'd just turned to step back to the counter, went straight up in the air, while Casper's went straight for his guns. The manager hit the floor. Taking cover behind the counter, Casper let off three shots before Blackman and his gang realized what was happening.

Two of the gang were sent reeling against a window of the bank and fell through it mortally wounded. The third shot whistled past Blackman's head and hit the guard outside who had just sprung to his feet. Blackman and Ace let rip a storm of rifle-lead in Casper's direction. Keeping it up, they both backed out of the bank on to the boardwalk. As they turned to make a dash for their horses, which the remaining two gang members were holding, Wright and McManus appeared on the scene with guns blazing. The two men holding the horses were killed. As they let drop the reins, the horses they were holding bolted and ran off down Main Street.

Blackman and Ace opened fire again, shooting wildly in all directions as they looked for somewhere to run. Casper, who had come to the front of the bank, had just started to fire at them when they spotted an alley down the side of the bank and dashed into it, firing rapidly as they went. Casper took cover by the entrance to the bank.

'Casper,' Wright called out, running to the boardwalk in front of the bank, 'you all right?'

'Yeah,' Casper called back in reply, realizing it was safe to step out of the bank. 'That was Blackman,' he said coming face to face with Wright. 'Where's he gone?'

'Down the alley,' Wright replied, pointing, as McManus suddenly appeared at his side.

As he spoke two horses with men on them suddenly stormed on to Main Street a few blocks away and rode furiously out of town. In a flash Casper, Wright and McManus ran to where a couple of horses were tied to a hitching rail. They jumped on to them and spurred them into a gallop in the direction Blackman and Ace had taken.

ELEVEN

'I thought you said Casper wasn't in town,' Blackman called to Ace as they fled across the open prairie.

'He wasn't,' Ace called back.

Blackman threw him a look of utter disdain and spurred his horse on harder than ever. There was no doubt in his mind that Casper would already be hot on their tails. He did not know the terrain but knew that Casper did. He began to fear that really now there was no escape.

'Which way is south?' he asked Ace.

Ace thought for a moment, looking about him. It was hard to gauge direction from a galloping horse, but he guessed it was about forty-five degrees east of the direction they were going.

'Thataway,' he said, pointing.

'Right,' replied Blackman. 'That's the way we're going. I've had enough of this God-forsaken territory!'

Looking over his shoulder, he could see Casper, Wright and McManus giving chase. They were still a good distance ahead of them but he knew they were unlikely to be able to maintain their lead indefinitely. He began to think that maybe he and Ace should separate. With a bit of luck it would be Ace that Casper followed rather than himself. He was about to suggest it, when a bullet zinged past him. Both he and Ace pulled their Colts at the same time and began to fire back. They rode on for a few minutes like this, sending lead and getting it back.

'Reckon we're gonna have to find some cover,' Ace called out.

Blackman agreed with him and looked about for a suitable place. Suddenly he caught sight of what looked like the opening of a canyon with a river running into its depths. In fact it was a ravine but one deep enough to serve their purposes.

'Over there,' he called to Ace, pulling his mount to the right.

'They're heading for Bailey's Gulch,' Casper called to Wright, spurring his horse harder. Bailey's Gulch was a geological freak in an area that was otherwise free of deep cuts in its terrain. It was almost big enough to pass for a canyon. Casper knew that if Blackman got into it and stayed in it, it could take them forever to flush him out. At its deepest it was a hundred feet to the bottom. Its sides were steep and there were plenty of slot canyons with places to hide and lie in ambush.

'We gonna be able to get out the other side?' Ace asked, as they raced into the mouth of the gulch.

'Shut up and just keep riding,' Blackman replied. He looked over his shoulder. As he knew they would, Casper and the others were following.

Casper called out to Wright to stick with him but told McManus to ride hard and come into the gulch from a slot further on. 'If they ride on through, just try and keep them pinned down 'til we join you. That's a Sharps,' he added, indicating a rifle in a holster attached to his horse's saddle. 'Use it.'

McManus reined off east, as Casper and Wright rode in to the gulch. Once in they quickly dismounted and began to pick their way forward gingerly on foot. Casper expected to find Blackman's and Ace's horses but they were nowhere to be seen. Except for the flow of the river, it was quiet and eerie and there was no sign of Blackman nor the man riding with him.

'Must have taken their mounts with them,' Wright remarked.

'It's wide enough,' Casper agreed. 'Just. More 'n' likely though sent them ahead. They came here to find cover.'

Casper knew the gulch well enough and reckoned he could guess where they would be hiding. Blackman would not be able to see them until they rounded a small bend a hundred yards up ahead. He and Wright inched their way forward, their guns drawn with triggers cocked. As they neared the spot Casper kept close to the gulch wall and stopped when they came to the bend. As he began to peer around it, a shot rang out, hitting the wall a few inches from his nose. He quickly pulled himself back behind cover.

'Just where I thought he'd be,' he remarked to Wright and then waited to hear if McManus was going to open fire. When he didn't, he hoped out loud he hadn't got lost.

'I don't think so,' Wright replied. 'He knows the

area almost as well as you do.'

They waited a few more minutes, then Casper said, 'Let's try it again.'

This time instead of giving cause for Blackman to open fire first, he put his Colt around the bend and fired a number of shots. As he reckoned, Blackman and Ace fired back twice as many, joined by the distinctive crack of the Sharps.

'Good,' Casper said. 'Now we've got them.'

The exchange of fire between McManus and Blackman and Ace went on for some minutes. Casper again peered around the bend and this time gunfire did not greet him.

'I'm gonna make a run for that crack over there,' he said to Wright, pointing to a fissure big enough to give a man cover in the wall opposite them a few yards ahead. 'When I say *now*, cover me.'

He fired a few shots. This started Blackman and Ace firing back. He waited for a lull in their return fire and then suddenly made a dash for the crack he'd pointed out to Wright.

'*Now*,' he said to Wright, as he went. Blackman and Ace saw him but too late.

Casper now had a clear picture of the slot canyon in which Blackman and Ace were hiding. He could see, too, the point from where McManus

had them pinned down. As long as he had ammunition enough it wouldn't be too difficult for him
to pick them off. He decided to give them a chance
to give themselves up.

'Blackman,' he called when the firing stopped.
'You're covered both sides. You don't stand a
chance. Throw your guns down.'

On hearing Casper call, Blackman pulled
himself tight in against the slot canyon wall. A
small boulder gave him some cover but he knew it
was not enough. Inwardly, he cursed the day he
had left Texas and again cursed Ace for getting it
wrong in Custer. He was so mad at him he could
have shot him himself there and then, But it *was*
Ace. He could curse him, but could he really kill
him after all they'd been through together? He
knew he couldn't. But there was something he
knew he had a right to ask him to do.

'Ace,' he said, 'we're finished however you look
at it. Our only chance is to make a dash up this
slot canyon.'

'Straight into that rifle fire,' Ace remarked,
indicating with his head the direction McManus's
fire was coming from.

'If we're lucky he won't get both of us,'
Blackman replied.

Ace was no fool and he knew what Blackman meant. Surrender was not part of their life-plan. He was both bad and mad enough to damn it all and go out in a blaze of glory. He also knew who it was Blackman would expect to be in the vanguard of that suicidal derring-do.

'What's it gonna be, Blackman?' Casper called out to them. 'You've got ten seconds to decide.'

Less than half of that time had passed when Casper sensed that something in the air was changing. He looked about him. Almost in the next instant McManus's body landed with a loud thump on the canyon floor between him and Blackman. McManus landed flat on his back and it was plain to see his throat had been cut from ear to ear, almost severing his head.

Indians, Casper thought to himself, looking up to see a few dozen of them standing at the top of the gulch, looking straight down at them.

Wright was stunned to see his sidekick of some time lying so horribly mutilated on the ground in front of him. He first thought was to open fire at the Indians high above them, but his second thought, as the discipline of being led by a brilliant and fearless leader began to kick in, was to await orders. Those orders were still forming in

Casper's mind. It didn't take long for them to take shape.

'Blackman,' he called out, 'I'd say your options suddenly became decidedly reduced.'

'I don't think so,' Blackman called back.

He had himself survived many times by flying in the face of impossible odds. The way he saw it now was that with the crossfire out of the way his path was clear to make an escape along the slot canyon he and Ace were in.

'Ace,' he said, 'when I give the word start firing at the Indians. They'll start firing back at all of us and that'll leave Casper either pinned down or dead. He's more exposed that we are. I'll make a run for it first and then you can follow.'

Ace wasn't convinced their chances of succeeding were that good, but equally he knew they didn't really have much choice in the matter.

'All right?' Blackman asked him.

'All right,' replied Ace. 'Just give the word.'

'Blackman,' Casper called out. 'You sure you seen what's above?'

'OK,' Blackman called back to Casper. 'You win. But I want some guarantees. Namely, that I get to keep my guns as long as we got a fight on our hands with the Indians. I give you my word I won't turn them on you.'

'Your word—' Casper began to call back but before he could finish his sentence Blackman had given Ace the order to start firing and he had let loose with a Winchester '72 at the Indians, who promptly returned fire.

'God damn it!' Casper exclaimed as he and Wright had to pull in tighter against the canyon walls to increase their cover. It was not, though, very effective against the fire that was raining down upon them. They both returned lead and a number of Indians fell. Wright took a flesh wound in an arm but was able to keep on firing.

The slot canyon along which Blackman and Ace were now making their escape provided enough cover from the overhang to make it nigh on impossible for the Indians to hit them. Casper, who was well aware of this, since he knew the gulch well, realized that to escape up that slot canyon was also the only hope he and Wright had. But their position was more exposed and it would be a risky business trying to make it into the slot canyon. Against this, though, their ammunition was not going to last for ever and then . . . a grisly death at the hands of the Indians. It was a prospect too dire to contemplate. McManus was lying there dead at their feet to remind them.

'Wright,' Casper called out, knowing he had been hit, 'we gotta make a dash for that slot canyon. You up to it? We'll have to move fast, one at a time.'

Wright had just called back an affirmative when he was hit again, this time in a thigh, the bullet shattering the bone. He fell to the ground, becoming an even easier target for Indian rifle-fire. Casper sprang into action. Miraculously surviving unscathed, he broke cover, grabbed Wright by the scruff of the neck and ran with him into the slot canyon. He didn't stop running until he knew they were out of sight to the Indians. Blackman, he knew, would be long gone by now. The Indians would be heading for the end of the slot canyon, which, while it would have offered Blackman a way out, meant a fairly steep climb with no horses at the end. His own and Wright's horses would, on the other hand, still be some-where round the mouth of the gulch.

'We might do better to go back,' he suggested to Wright.

'Casper, don't wait for me,' Wright said, between stabs of pain, looking down at his thigh wound. 'I'm losing blood fast.'

'Don't be stupid,' Casper was adamant. 'I ain't leaving you here, if there's any chance those savages will get their hands on you. Now just shut up and save your strength.'

He pulled a bandanna from his neck and tied a tourniquet around Wright's thigh. Then he looked at the flesh wound in his arm. It was minor enough to ignore and there was little blood. He looked around him, deciding what to do next. All firing had ceased and it was again eerily silent.

'I'm gonna go and get the horses while those Indians are occupied with Blackman,' he said to Wright.

'Casper, forget about me,' Wright said again, his voice weak. 'I'm finished. You ain't. Just go, escape while you can.'

Casper knew what Wright was saying made sense, but he had never left a man to die alone before and he wasn't about to start now. Besides which, there was still the possibility the Indians would get to him, and he wasn't going to risk that any more than he had to.

'I told you, I ain't leaving you. If we're lucky, I got time to get to the horses and bring one back for you and that's what I'm gonna do. Now you just lie there with this at the ready.' Casper placed Wright's Winchester, fully reloaded, at his side, and his Colt .45 in his right hand. 'You'll stand a good chance if any Indians come down there,' he indicated the path leading out of the slot canyon. 'I'll be back before you know it.'

With that he turned and hurried off in the direction of the main canyon. As he got there, he heard gunfire. It was coming from up above and he knew it could only mean that the Indians had found Blackman and his fellow long rider.

Good! he thought, it would keep them occupied while he went to find their horses.

TWELVE

The attempted robbery of the town bank had left Sheriff Mailer uncomfortably undecided about what he should do. When he'd heard gun shots he'd come running from his office just in time to see Casper, Wright and McManus riding fast out of town after the bank robbers. He was relieved to find all the fatalities were on the outlaws' side and that the security guard at the bank wasn't seriously injured. He'd calmed things down and the town quickly returned to normal. What worried him, though, was the fact that as the town sheriff he should have mounted a posse and joined Casper in his attempts to hunt down the gang. But he knew that wouldn't have been what Casper wanted. He liked to do things his way.

Nevertheless, he felt he should not be sitting in his office twiddling his thumbs wondering how things were going out on the prairie. He decided the least he should do was to ride out and scout around a bit. Leaving his deputy in charge, he armed himself with what he thought might be necessary and decided to call in on the doctor's to see how Tom Hart, the security guard, an old friend of his, was doing before hitting the trail.

He found Hart being patched up by Dr Reid, having had a slug extracted from a wound close to his heart.

'How's it going, Doctor?' he asked, entering Dr Reid's surgery.

'He'll live,' replied the doctor, 'though he's a lucky man.'

They exchanged a few words about the robbery and then Sheriff Mailer asked how Mary Baylis was doing. Dr Reid had begun to tell him, when his wife came in from the back room where the widow was being looked after.

'Sheriff Mailer,' she said, 'I'm glad you're here.' She told him that Mary had tried to warn Casper about the bank being robbed.

'What?' the sheriff asked incredulously.

'It seems that the gang held the family at gun-

142

point for a few days but left just before the Indians attacked. She also said they'd only been gone a short while when the Indians attacked and that they must have been close enough to come back and do something to help but obviously chose not to. This has upset her more than them holding the family at gun-point. She thinks her husband might not have died if they'd come back and helped.'

'My God!' exclaimed Mailer, 'could any man sink lower than to leave an innocent family to the mercy of a bunch of renegade Indians? Can I speak to her?'

'Later. She's sleeping again now. My husband had to give her more laudanum to settle her down after what she had to tell us. She said the gang planned the robbery while holding the family captive.'

'God dammit!' Sheriff Mailer exclaimed again. Then he told Mrs Reid and her husband that he was riding out to help Casper catch the gang. He took his leave of them and told the doctor's wife to assure the widow that the gang were not going to get away with it; that once Casper knew what had happened he'd certainly make sure of that.

Casper had been wrong in assuming that the
gunfire he heard was the sound of Blackman and
the Indians fighting it out. It was the army
suddenly appearing and opening fire on the
Indians. They had been on patrol a couple of miles
east, when they heard the sound of gunfire and
had decided to investigate. It was only as the
sound of gunfire intensified that he began to real-
ize that it wasn't necessarily as he had thought,
that Blackman and the Indians could not be
making that much noise. It never occurred to him
it might be the army again coming to their rescue.
If anything, he thought it must have been Sheriff
Mailer with a posse seeking to help track down
Blackman.

Hurrying on, he made his way to the mouth of
the gulch and found the horses nearby grazing on
green grass near the small river that flowed into
the gulch. Swinging up on to his own mount, he
grabbed the reins of the other and rode back
towards the gulch. By now the sound of gunfire
was beginning to fade. He would have liked to go
to see who it was that had joined in the affray but
decided he could not risk leaving Wright in so
dangerous a situation while there was still the
possibility of Indians finding him. Just one of

them could put him through an awful lot of agony.

He found Wright still alive but weak from loss of blood.

'Come on,' he said, helping him on to his horse, 'we'll ride back to Custer. But before that, something's been going on out there and I aim to find out what.'

'What do mean, something's been going on?' Wright asked, as he sat as best he could on his saddle. 'I thought there seemed a dang lot of gunfire.'

'I don't know exactly,' Casper replied. 'Reckon you'll be able to hang on?'

'Yeah,' Wright replied, making himself secure enough to ride.

As they cleared the mouth of the gulch Casper caught sight of the army near where he knew the slot canyon rose.

'So that's it,' he said to Wright. 'Reckon we've been in luck again.'

They rode to where soldiers were checking over the Indian dead and found the lieutenant they'd last seen riding away from the Baylis farm. It didn't take Casper long to ascertain that there were no white civilians among the dead.

He told the lieutenant about the attempted

bank robbery in Custer and his pursuit of Blackman and a surviving member of his gang to the gulch and the subsequent attack by the Indians.

'Thought the Indians might have done for Blackman and the other villain, but looking about here it seems they didn't get them after all.'

'So that's who they were,' the lieutenant remarked. 'I thought I saw a couple of men ride off as we approached but until now I haven't had a chance to give it any thought. Guess I thought they were just keeping on running to escape the Indians.'

'Which way they go?' Casper asked.

The lieutenant looked around him trying to get his bearings and then pointed. 'That way, east,' he informed Casper.

'OK, thanks, lieutenant,' Casper replied. 'Think you can look after Wright? I got some unfinished business to attend to.'

'Course we can, but don't you. . . ?' the lieutenant sounded doubtful.

'No,' replied Casper. 'Reckon it's best if I go alone. I know this country well. Hunting a few men won't be no more difficult than hunting wild animals, and that's done best on your own. Take

Wright into Custer. You'll find the Baylis widow there in the doctor's infirmary.'

The lieutenant began to ask him for more news about Mary Baylis but was cut short by Sheriff Mailer's riding in amongst them. He'd ridden some distance out of Custer when he'd heard gunfire and worked out where it was coming from.

'Will, you all night?' he asked, looking at the dead Indians lying all around.

'Yeah,' Casper replied. 'Thanks to the lieutenant here and his men.'

'And what about Blackman?'

'Got away, again,' Casper replied.

The sheriff told Casper and the lieutenant about what the doctor's wife had told him Mary Baylis had said and their reactions were as outraged as would be expected from any self-respecting men. The lieutenant wanted to start right away after Blackman but was persuaded by Casper that it'd be better if he went after them alone.

'They'll have headed up into the hills and will have more chance of dodging a company of soldiers than of being caught. I know this country, I'll get 'em. Wright needs to see a doctor. Best you and the sheriff here take him into Custer.'

147

'Uh-uh,' insisted Sheriff Mailer, 'I'm coming with you, Will. That vermin robbed my bank. It's my job to make 'em pay for it.'

Casper knew when not to argue with a man and agreed to Mailer going with him.

Blackman and Ace looked around and saw that no one was on their tail. They pulled up.

'Couldn't've turned out better,' Ace remarked, holding the reins of his horse tight.

'It ain't over yet,' Blackman replied, looking back long and hard in the direction from which they had just come. In front of them the ground was rising and becoming more thickly wooded. 'Reckon the best we can do is head for Texas. If the Indians didn't do for Casper and whoever it was that was with him, he'll soon be on our backs again. Don't reckon we can count on the army coming to our rescue every time we need 'em.'

Ace smiled and then said: 'It's a long ride, Dunc.'

'Got any better ideas?' Blackman snapped in reply. 'If you'd done better in Custer, we wouldn't be in this mess now.'

'I told you that Casper was not in town when I left there the day before yesterday. If he had've been I'd have seen him. There ain't even much of a stagecoach office there, so what was he doing there?'

'Looking for us, you dolt-head, which he is gonna keep on doing – and which is why we're clearing out of the territory,' was Blackman's terse answer. 'Come on,' he said, spurring his horse to carry on riding eastward.

Casper and Mailer didn't have any trouble picking up Blackman's tracks. They were heading east out of the Black Hills, this was obvious. Casper reckoned they'd keep on riding until nightfall and then camp somewhere.

'You reckon?' Mailer asked.

'Ain't nowhere else they can go now,' Casper replied.

As they criss-crossed the country he knew so well, it wasn't long before he and Mailer caught sight of them. By this time night was falling and it was only because they were on high ground that they were able to spot the two outlaws down below. Mailer was all for riding hell for leather at them, but Casper's way was to stalk them. They did so until it was almost dark and then watched them rein in their mounts and make camp.

'Reckon this is as good a spot as any,' Blackman said to Ace.

'There doesn't seem to be any sign of anyone following us,' Ace said, dismounting. 'Maybe the Indians got them after all. They would have had a clear view of them from where they stood.'

'Don't count on it,' was all Blackman said.

After stretching their legs for a few moments, they set about unsaddling their horses. Once that job was done, Ace began to collect wood to make a fire. Blackman thought of telling him not to, but decided it was probably safe enough. And besides, he was hungry and thirsty. There was coffee, beans and beef jerky in their saddle-bags. If these vittals were not what he'd reckoned on feeding on that night, he decided not to deny them to himself, using the excuse that if Casper or anyone had been on their tail he'd have spotted them by now.

Casper and Mailer took up a position among trees on ground above the two outlaws. Casper wished he'd been alone and mounted on his own horse Digger. Digger knew when to be quiet, when to

not even let out the merest snort, but the mount
he'd commandeered in Custer could not be relied
upon. It seemed intelligent and to have taken to
him well enough, but he didn't know it and so
could not take any risks that it wouldn't make a
noise and let his position out. He knew nothing of
whether or not the sheriff's bay could be relied
upon.

'Reckon we ought to tie the horses up some
distance away,' he whispered to Maller, telling
him why.

The fire Ace had built crackled away. This and
the noise he and Blackman made as they went
about making camp and getting the meal ready
were enough to keep them from hearing any
sounds Casper and Mailer might have made in
getting the horses out of the way. They had no
idea their pursuers were so close. Casper was not
one for taking prisoners. Mailer being the law and
being present did not alter this fact one iota. As
far as Casper was concerned the law could not be
counted upon to deal with scum fittingly. And
Blackman and Ace, after what Mailer had told
him they'd done to the Baylis family in running
off to leave them to the savagery of Indians, were
lower than a snake's belly. Besides which, it was

too much bother to take in men who'd grab any opportunity to try and escape. If there was a reward on their heads, better to haul them in dead. If there wasn't, better to plant them in some remote part and say nothing.

There was a reward for Blackman and his gang, but Casper hadn't yet figured out how best to take him and the surviving rider who was with him. He'd sleep on it, he thought, and make a decision before dawn. Mailer had brought some chuck with him, but they didn't make a fire upon which to cook it. Instead they chewed on strips of beef jerky and washed it down with water from a stream.

'Reckon there's any Indians in the neighbourhood?' Ace asked Blackman, as they sat in front of a fiercely burning log fire eating their meal.

'Who knows?' Blackman replied. 'Even if there are, they don't usually attack at night, at least not as far as I've heard. Ain't ever had much to do with Indians before I came to Dakota. Texas Rangers, yes. But Indians, no.'

'Sure hope you're right about them not attacking at night,' Ace remarked, drinking the last of his coffee. 'Suppose I'll turn in then. Gonna be chilly, I think. Glad I've got my bedroll.'

Blackman merely grunted in reply. He was busy building himself a smoke. He was dog-tired but didn't feel completely safe yet. The William D. Caspers of this world did not give up so easily. The only thing that really stopped them dead in their tracks was death itself He wished he knew whether or not the Indians had killed him back there in the gulch. With the question having to go unanswered but filling his head, he finished his cigarette, got into his bedroll and lay awake staring at the fire, which was beginning to burn down.

'Ace,' he said.

Getting no answer he called out his name again, this time louder.

'What do you want?' Ace, who'd fallen straight to sleep the moment he'd pulled the canvas of the bedroll up to his chin, answered.

'Put some more wood on the fire,' Blackman ordered him. 'Don't want to get eaten in the night by wild animals.'

You do it, Ace almost replied, but thought better of it.

In the hour before dawn, Casper decided what he was going to do. He waited, however, until daylight began to break before acting upon it.

Mailer was still asleep. Thinking this was just as well, Casper stealthily crept down the hill towards the outlaws' camp until he was close enough to be able to see the two men lying asleep in their bedrolls. As he looked one of them stirred; whether Blackman or Ace he didn't know, or care. He waited to see if the man awoke. When he didn't, he crept up to him and holding a Colt against his forehead cocked the trigger. His eyes opened instantly and he sat up. It was Ace.

'Don't move an inch,' Casper said to him. 'Or you're a dead man.'

Before Ace was able to take in what had happened, Blackman was awake and reaching for his own Colt. Going into a roll he fired, hitting Ace in the stomach. Casper fired back, wounding him in the chest. Both outlaws lay on the ground, blood pouring from their wounds. Casper stood up, looking down at them. He'd planned to string them up, but reckoned the way they were going to die now would be painful enough.

'Oh God . . . oh God . . . !' Ace began to moan, holding his stomach and stirring up the dying embers of the fire with his legs.

'Son of a bitch!' Blackman groaned, beginning to recover himself a bit.

When the impact of the bullet sent him reeling he had lost his gun. Now he felt around in the dirt trying to find it. Casper walked over to him, saw the gun and kicked it away. He had already disarmed Ace. As he stood staring down contemptuously at both of them, Mailer came racing down the hill.

'Don't reckon they'll be holding up any more stagecoaches or robbing any more banks,' he said to him. 'Nor leaving any more women and children to be raped and mutilated by redskins. Don't know whether to scalp them, finish them off or just let them die like the animals they are.'

'Why didn't you wake me?' Mailer asked.

'There weren't no need,' was all Casper said in reply.

When Blackman saw that the man who had appeared amongst them was wearing a badge, he felt somehow relieved. Not that the sheriff could have in anyway saved him. His life was ebbing away. He was not afraid, only angry with himself for letting Casper creep up on them the way he had. If anything stopped him from doing something as terrifying as scalping them, he knew it would only be the presence of the law.

'Reckon I'll just go and get saddled up, then, and come back for you two later,' Casper said.

No sound except the suffering of agony came from either Ace or Blackman. Ace knew his Winchester was nearby. In his mind he began to move towards it, but in reality he still lay on the ground writhing in pain, his hands pressing down on his wound. Blackman was choking on his own blood.

'If you're still alive when I get back I'll cook you up some breakfast,' were the last words either of them heard from Casper, as he turned and began to make his way back to the clump of trees he'd camped in.

Two days later he and Mailer rode into Custer, with the bodies of the two outlaws tied to their horses, and headed straight for Mailer's office. As people saw them they stopped and stared. Their scrutiny made Sheriff Mailer feel self-conscious but Casper barely noticed their presence. His eyes were fixed straight ahead. Towns were not places he liked. The people in them, he figured, just didn't really know.

At the far end of Main Street could be seen the white tents of the army. The lieutenant had decided to stay put and see what the outcome of Casper's pursuit of the road agents would be. He stepped out of Dr Reid's surgery and appeared on the boardwalk as Mailer and Casper rode by. Seeing him, Casper turned his horse to face him and stopped.

'I see you got them,' the lieutenant remarked, nodding his head in the direction of the two outlaws slung across their horses. Flies quickly began to buzz about them.

'Said I would,' Casper replied. 'How's Wright?'

'Alive but the doctor couldn't save his leg.'

'And the widow?'

'She'll feel better now, knowing you got them,' the lieutenant replied.

'Tell her they died like the animals they were,' Casper said, turning and continuing down the street. Watching him go, the lieutenant wondered if it was the kind of thing a lady should hear. Casper dismounted outside the sheriff's office and tied his horse to the hitching rail.

Mailer was inside talking to his deputy. 'Better get those to the undertaker,' he said to him, on seeing Casper pull up outside and come in, 'before they begin to stink the town out.'

'Sure thing, Sheriff,' the deputy replied, looking at Casper with awe as he passed him to leave the office.

Casper stretched his legs and took a coffee poured for him by Mailer from a pot on the stove.

'Reckon the bank will have reopened?' Casper asked.

'Sure to have,' Mailer replied.

'Good, I got some unfinished business to attend to,' Casper said, pulling the winnings from his gambling with the half-breed out of a pocket inside his buckskins.

'Kept meaning to ask you if they tried to rob the bank before you had time to deposit it,' Mailer remarked. 'Folks'll think you're a real hero, if you go ahead and deposit that after what's happened.'

'Well, folks is stupid,' Casper replied.

'They all know what you were doing in the bank when Blackman tried to rob it. So will Mary Baylis by now.'

Casper looked pained. 'Yeah, well. . . .' was all he said.

2